"There is only one Black Domino!"

Diana was adamant. "England could easily spare a dozen like me."

"It is blasphemous to suggest there are dozens like you," the Domino replied gallantly, his voice low with passion. "I have never met another . . . not with brown eyes so lustrous or skin as soft as a rose," he said, bending his head to brush her lips.

Diana knew she should draw away, but it was impossible. She had dreamed of this moment a thousand times. Her mouth opened to receive his kisses, but nothing in her dreams had prepared her for the rush of passion that flooded her body.

The Domino was startled at the warmth of her response. He had kept a succession of mistresses, but not one of them had ever kissed him with such pure, unbridled enjoyment.

Diana's eyes fluttered open, hazy with desire. "I never knew . . . a kiss could make one feel quite so . . . so wonderful."

He could not help himself; his arms tightened around her.

Regency England: 1811-1820

"It was the best of times, it was the worst of times...."
As George III languished in madness, the pampered and profligate Prince of Wales led the land in revelry and the elegant Beau Brummel set the style. Across the Channel, Napoleon continued to plot against the English until his final exile to St. Helena. Across the Atlantic, America renewed hostilities with an old adversary, declaring war on Britain in 1812. At home, Society glittered, love matches abounded and poets such as Lord Byron flourished. It was a time of heroes and villains, a time of unrelenting charm and gaiety, when entire fortunes were won or lost on a turn of the dice and reputation was all. A dazzling period that left its mark on two continents and whose very name became a byword for elegance and romance.

Books by Jeanne Carmichael

MADCAP
JOHNNY

JEANNE CARMICHAEL

Harlequin Books

TORONTO • NEW YORK • LONDON
AMSTERDAM • PARIS • SYDNEY • HAMBURG
STOCKHOLM • ATHENS • TOKYO • MILAN
MADRID • WARSAW • BUDAPEST • AUCKLAND

Published January 1993

ISBN 0-373-31190-7

MADCAP JOHNNY

CHAPTER ONE

LORD JOHNNY DRAYTON paused on the wide marble
steps of the magnificent staircase leading down to the
Great Hall and grinned at the chaotic confusion below
him. Sounds of indignation and irate protests filled the
air. The angry voice of his host, Louis Chevron, was the
loudest.

"It is an outrage! By whose authority do you act?
Need I remind you that we are no longer at war with
England and these gentlemen are my honoured guests?"

The French lieutenant squared his shoulders and lifted
a stubborn chin. "My orders are to capture the Black
Domino at all costs—"

"Then go and do it!" Louis interrupted rudely above
the murmurs of astonishment from his guests—those
who understood enough French to catch the reference to
the infamous spy. The slender, dark-haired Louis was
normally the soul of grace and courtesy, but now his dark
eyes burned with passionate rage and he spoke wildly.
"You'll not find that devil here. Do you think I would
entertain such a one? Bah! You insult me and you insult
my guests."

"We shall inconvenience them as little as possible," the
lieutenant replied, glancing about. "Certainly they have
nothing to fear if they are, as you claim, entirely innocent."

Johnny judged it time to make his entrance. He made a play of straightening the lace at his wrists as he casually strolled down the remaining steps and hailed his host.

"Louis, my dear friend, I protest. You did not tell me theatricals were to be performed this morning. What play is this?"

Chevron turned and, with an angry emphatic gesture towards the lieutenant, said, "This imbecile wants to search all the gentlemen and their rooms. He thinks to find the Black Domino among my guests. Can you conceive of such idiocy? I am embarrassed to face you, my lord."

Johnny tossed back his head and laughed, causing a curly lock of black hair to fall across his wide brow. His bright blue eyes danced with amusement. "Oh, ho! The Black Domino here? It is a farce, then?" He looked round at his fellow guests. The ladies had withdrawn to one side of the huge room and the gentlemen stood in a tight knot. His eyes picked out Lord Claypool and he grinned. "What say you, Basil? Been keeping secrets from us?"

"It is no laughing matter, Johnny," the rotund little Englishman replied. "The officer is deadly serious and suspects us all."

"Then either the deeds of the Black Domino have been grossly exaggerated, or the good lieutenant is near blind," Johnny said. "With the best will in the world, old fellow, I cannot imagine you swinging from a tree to unseat a French courier as I have heard the Domino did!"

There was a general chorus of laughter, and Basil himself joined in, patting his protruding belly. "Lord, it would be enough to kill a fellow were I to hit him with this!"

The lieutenant was plainly unappreciative and motioned to two of his men. "Enough of this nonsense. We will search the rooms at once."

"I beg your pardon, sir," Johnny offered with a show of contriteness. "I fear I've offended you, but surely you can see the jest? Why, Lord Claypool will entertain his friends at home for months telling them how he was suspected of being the notorious Black Domino."

"I am delighted it affords you amusement, sir, but to me it is hardly a matter for jesting. A French courier was attacked less than four miles from here this morning and vital papers stolen from him. Every house in the area is being searched. I have my orders."

"Attacked? Good heavens! Was the courier hurt?"

"No," Lieutenant Jennot admitted reluctantly, thinking of the poor fellow left stranded in the road in his unmentionables. "But it is a serious matter, all the same."

"Of course, and I offer my abject apologies and place myself at your service. It would be most lamentable if this infamous fellow were to strain the relations between our two great nations. Gad, it was devilishly dull when France was closed to Englishmen. And as for clothing—well, sir, you would hardly credit the lengths we were put to trying to dress creditably. Those who play at blasted politics have no consideration for the rest of us." Johnny turned to Louis Chevron and placed a compelling hand on his sleeve. "Louis, *mon cher,* we must do what we can to accommodate the lieutenant. May I have your leave to escort him personally?"

His host shrugged. "As you will, my lord, but the notion is ludicrous, and an insult to my house."

"Whose room do you desire to see first, Lieutenant? May I offer mine?" Johnny asked with the excited air of a small boy setting off on an adventure. His eyes lit with mischievous humour and he added innocently, "Then, perhaps, Lady Throckmorton's?"

"Over my dead body," the elderly lady threatened. Her massive bosom, draped in swathes of majestic purple, heaved as she turned to face the lieutenant. She addressed him in fluent French, and what her voice lacked in proper accent was made up for with the wide range of her vocabulary. The oaths she hurled at him were the sort one heard on the docks and turned his ears a bright red.

"No, no," the lieutenant hastened to assure her, taking an involuntary step backwards. "If the ladies will remain together belowstairs, it will not be necessary to search their apartments."

"I should hope not," Lady Throckmorton said, and turned to her daughter, a thinner, paler version of herself who stood with flushed face and downcast eyes. "Come, Violet. The air grows putrid in here. We shall wait in the garden until these creatures have left. Come along, Diana."

Diana Talbot rose obediently and followed her mother and grandmother from the room. She was a tall young woman, beyond the first blush of youth but not quite on the shelf. She passed close to Lord John and her fine brown eyes raked over him with a measure of contempt as she spoke softly to her mother. "Obviously the lieutenant is mistaken. There is not a man of mettle amongst this entire lot, much less one of the calibre of the Black Domino. I am glad we return home tomorrow."

"Hush, Diana!" her mother hissed sharply.

"Oh, leave her be," Lady Throckmorton said. "Likely the gel is right. A more frivolous set of gentlemen I've never seen," she added, her deep voice carrying clearly as she sailed out the door and into the garden.

Johnny grinned at Miss Talbot's retreating, and very shapely, figure. "A pity the young lady is so sober-minded," he confided to the lieutenant. "I fear she views my idleness with less than compassion and admires not my sartorial splendour, though I thought this coat particularly becoming. I had it made up in Paris, you know." He turned so that the officer might admire the long tails of his pale yellow morning coat.

The lieutenant stared at him for half a moment before spinning abruptly on his heel. "Keep the gentlemen and ladies confined to this room and the gardens," he ordered three of his men and motioned for two others to follow him up the stairs.

"Allow me to show you the way," Johnny said, easily catching up with him. "My chamber is just at the end of the hall." There was no reply and they walked up the steps in silence for a moment. "Tell me, Lieutenant, what makes you think the Black Domino might be lurking about here? One would think that if he robbed your courier this morning, he would be well on his way to England by now."

"The roads are all blocked and every Englishman leaving Calais is being thoroughly searched. If he is, you may be assured he will not slip through our fingers this time."

"Well, I hope you catch him soon. It makes travelling most uncomfortable for the rest of us. The Custom House is bad enough without all this additional searching." Johnny paused before a door and with his hand on the knob warned, "My valet will not take kindly to your men tumbling my clothes about or disarranging my luggage."

He received another glare for his efforts and hastily opened the door.

Jenkins looked up in surprise at their entrance. He was in the midst of packing a large valise laid open upon the bed. Several shirts and stocks could be seen neatly folded but it was the trunk on the floor that interested the lieutenant. Jenkins stepped quickly in front of it and dropped the dressing-gown he'd been folding over its contents.

"Stand aside there," the lieutenant ordered, striding into the room.

The man folded his muscular arms and continued to stand guard over the trunk.

"I am afraid he does not speak French," Johnny said apologetically. "Allow me. Jenkins, move aside. It's quite all right. The lieutenant here is seeking a terrible bandit—"

"Spy," the French officer corrected and motioned to one of his men to inspect the trunk.

Several cloaks were removed and then the young officer grinned broadly, holding up a bottle of brandy. "There must be above a dozen more bottles in here," he told the lieutenant.

"You do understand how it is," Johnny said, with a delicate shrug of his shoulders. "One simply cannot get decent brandy in England. Of course I intended to declare it at the Custom House—"

"Your small efforts at smuggling do not concern me," the lieutenant broke in coldly. He ordered every item of clothing removed, the pockets turned out and the linings thoroughly searched.

Jenkins watched them through narrowed eyes and under his unrelenting stare, his young master's clothing was treated with respect. But he was unable to stop them from examining every inch of the trunk and valise; even his lordship's boots were inspected for secret hiding places.

Johnny watched for a few moments, his amusement apparent, and then strolled out on the balcony. Lady Throckmorton, her daughter and granddaughter were seated in the small courtyard below. Lady Pennington and her maid had joined them and a young French officer stood discreetly just outside the garden doors.

He saw Diana Talbot glance up and bowed in her direction. She quite deliberately turned her shoulder to him. And a very pretty shoulder it was, he thought, continuing to watch her. The broad-brimmed hat she wore hid her chestnut curls and shielded her delicate rose-and-white complexion from his view, but he knew well enough the sculpted lines of her features to sketch them from memory. Miss Talbot was a most striking young lady.

And wishes nothing to do with you, my lad, he reminded himself. The lady had made that much abundantly clear during the past week. Her first rebuff to what he thought had been a rather prettily phrased compliment had startled him, and despite his most ingenious attempts, she had remained determinedly cool towards him. Louis had told him privately that Miss Talbot had lost a young man she had been strongly attached to during Wellington's campaign at Vittoria. Their engagement had not been official, but, Louis had explained, shrugging his expressive shoulders, it had been expected. Johnny had comprehended. He had also learned from Claypool that her father had died some years previously during a skirmish on the Peninsula. Miss Talbot's heart was given to the military, and she had nothing but marked contempt for fashionable young gentlemen.

He was abruptly recalled from his thoughts by the French lieutenant who politely requested him to step into the room and remove his close-fitting coat. Johnny good-

naturedly obliged and maintained an air of one humour-
ing a recalcitrant child. His sunny temperament seemed
to annoy the lieutenant, who curtly ordered him to take
off his boots.

"Come now, is that really necessary?" Johnny asked.
"It takes poor Jenkins hours to obtain a shine such as
this," he pointed out, displaying a glossy black Hessian.
"Let us be reasonable, Lieutenant. No man of sense
would walk about with valuable papers secreted in his
boots. *Mon Dieu!* Can you not conceive how uncomfortable it would be?"

"The boots, if you please, sir."

Johnny sighed and motioned to his valet, for it was
near impossible to remove his footwear without assistance. When at last he stood in his stocking feet, he spun
round in front of the lieutenant. "Well, sir? Would you
have me disrobe further?"

The officer observed him without any outward show
of emotion. It was quite apparent, even to a less discerning eye, that nothing could be hidden on Lord John's
body. His smallclothes were moulded to his figure. Even
the tiniest scrap of paper would have been noticeable.

"You may dress," the lieutenant said, lighting a cigar
while he watched the young lord. He blew a cloud of
smoke and then added, rather casually, "I am most impressed, my lord. You are singularly muscular for a gentleman who leads such an indolent life."

Johnny's head was turned as his valet assisted him into
his coat and for a brief second the blue eyes hardened and
the muscles about the wide mouth tightened. But it was
only for a second. When he faced the officer again, he
was grinning. "Indolent? I take issue with you, sir. I am
a superb horseman, box with the best of them and when
I am home, fence daily. Are you perhaps a student of the

art, Lieutenant?'' he asked, his eyes on the sword at the officer's side. "I find it marvellous for keeping one's muscles from growing flabby.''

"And that is an object with you, my lord?''

"But of course. It is imperative if one's clothes are to fit well. I would have thought that as a Frenchman you would understand. Only observe how well this coat sets—''

"I fancy you fence with more than swords, my lord,'' the lieutenant interrupted and gestured impatiently to his man. "Come, we must search the other rooms.''

Johnny followed him out into the hall and watched the lieutenant enter Lord Claypool's room. Jenkins stood beside him and when the door had closed on the officer, he looked up at his master. "Do you think he suspects—''

"Hush!'' Johnny warned in a quick whisper and then spoke more normally, "Finish packing, Jenkins. I grow weary of France with all her secret agents and officious soldiers. I think it is well we leave this afternoon.''

But Johnny, along with the rest of Louis Chevron's guests, had to cool his heels in the Great Hall until the French officer completed his search. It took nearly two hours.

The lieutenant, for all his diligence, was unable to unearth anything the least bit incriminating in any of the gentlemen's effects. He would have given a month's pay to have been allowed to search the ladies' apartments, as well, but that would have created an uproar even he was unprepared to deal with. It did not stop him, however, from lecturing the assembled guests before he departed.

He was not of a height that commanded attention, and he chose to stand on the third step of the grand staircase, that he might look down on the English. Reluctantly, he addressed them in their own language.

"I must warn you that should any of you attempt to harbour, or to in any way aid, the spy known as the Black Domino, your actions will be construed by the French government to be that of treason and you will be treated accordingly."

Miss Audley, companion to Lady Pennington, spoiled the effect with a nervous titter. "Oh, dear me, but we've no notion of what the gentleman even looks like. How would one know?"

There was loud nervous laughter from a few of the gentlemen present and Lady Pennington sighed heavily at the foolishness of the girl, but the lieutenant chose to take her seriously.

"From various reports, we know this man to be above average height," he paused, glancing about the hall. "Rather like Lord John Drayton," he added coldly. "And of similar build. Might I enquire your age, my lord?"

"Nine-and-twenty," Johnny returned promptly from his seat near the fire. He lounged at ease, his long, booted legs stretched out in front of him. "Should you like me to stand?" he asked helpfully.

"That will not be necessary. To answer you, miss, the gentleman in question is of similar height, weight and age to Lord John. Rumour has it the spy has golden hair, though of course that could be merely the effects of a wig. There are no known distinguishing marks. He is reputed to be completely fearless and an expert marksman."

"That lets out Lord John, then," Percy Montbalm murmured, casting a sly glance at Drayton. "Gad, I recollect how nervous you was when that fellow at the inn asked you to step outside, 'cause his sister kept making sheep's eyes at you. Quaking in your boots, you were!''

"Oh, come, my dear Montbalm. The brute was twice my size and expressed a distinct desire to rearrange my features. Now, had he agreed to box like a civilised gentleman—"

"You forget yourselves," Lady Throckmorton interrupted ominously. She stood, and after quelling Montbalm with a stare, turned to face the lieutenant. "Are you quite finished, sir? You have already delayed our journey and now we will of necessity be on the road in the evening. I warn you, Lieutenant, should our carriage be set upon, your superiors shall hear of this." She advanced towards the steps as she spoke.

"My apologies for the inconvenience, my lady. I will send an armed escort with you, should you desire it. However, save for the Black Domino, the road is perfectly safe. Now, if you will allow me, I have only one more announcement and then you may be on your way." He paused, waiting until he had the complete attention of all those gathered. When the room was quiet, he said, "That you should realise the seriousness with which the government views the activities of the Black Domino, I will tell you that a reward of twenty thousand pounds has been posted for information that leads to the arrest of this spy."

"Twenty thousand," Violet Talbot breathed softly and glanced swiftly at her daughter. Lord, that was enough to purchase a small cottage—one well away from her mother's domineering hand.

Percy Montbalm whistled through his teeth and Lord Claypool's loud voice carried clearly, "Egad! If I were the Domino, I'd be tempted to turn myself in and collect the reward. Twenty thousand—it's unheard of!''

Diana Talbot stirred uneasily. She misliked the astonishment greeting the lieutenant's news. Not that she believed any Englishman would betray another to the
French, not for any price—but she could feel the tension
in the room and twenty thousand was a small fortune.

LADY THROCKMORTON'S PARTY was the first to leave.
She declined the offer of an escort from the lieutenant,
from Lord John and even from poor Lord Claypool. She
was irritable and testy over the long delay and considered the lot of them fools. She told the lieutenant pointedly that if his men had not been able to catch one spy
when he was known to be in the neighbourhood, it was
highly unlikely they would afford her any protection
against a gang of thieves.

Lord John's offer she considered only momentarily.
He was a handsome devil, but all the world knew he was
a hardened bachelor. It was highly unlikely a girl of four-
and-twenty would be able to bring him up to scratch
when he'd not succumbed to the charms of the countless
younger ladies who had set their caps for him. It was true
Diana had shown no interest in him thus far, but the boy
did possess a certain charm of manner, and Lady
Throckmorton would not wager a farthing on Diana being proof against it were she to continue seeing him. No,
she wanted her granddaughter suitably married and not
languishing after some care-for-nobody. Lord John's
offer was dismissed out of hand.

Claypool received a contemptuous sniff and the brunt
of her tongue, for she was out of patience with him. The
whole purpose of bringing Diana abroad was to give the
girl a chance to become better acquainted with Claypool, but he had mismanaged the entire affair. Pressed
her too hard, Lady Throckmorton thought, though she'd

warned him to go gently. Diana had rejected his suit the evening before, and nothing her grandmother or her mother had said made the slightest difference. Whistled a tidy fortune down the wind, the chit had, and with as much unconcern as though she'd dozens of offers to choose from. Lady Throckmorton's temper rose again at the very thought of it, and she took her leave of Louis Chevron with less than good grace.

Louis stood dejectedly at the door and Johnny clapped an arm about his shoulders. "Cheer up, my friend. Lady Throckmorton is a termagant. Why, in London, it is considered a mark of distinction to receive one of her scolds."

Chevron smiled, but it was a sad effort and did not quite reach his eyes. "I hope you will not allow this unpleasantness to prejudice you against France, my lord. Not all of us view the English with the animosity of the military. I fear my cousin will never forgive me if you have taken offence, and I have looked forward to seeing her again after all these years."

"Juliana? Never worry. She has been plaguing my brother to bring her over for a visit and Spencer can deny her nothing. Especially now that she has given him an heir."

"I pray you are right. She is all the family I have left now and I am most anxious to see the babe. He bears my name, you know," he added proudly, a pleased light in his dark eyes.

"I know," Johnny said, laughing. "We share the honour. John Louis Drayton, Viscount Thornley. Quite a handle for such a wee fellow, but he is not yet aware of all his dignity. You will find him charming."

"As you do? Tell me, my lord, do you not feel any resentment that he has, how do you say, usurped your place?"

"Ha!" Johnny snorted and grinned. "My brother is so delighted to have an heir that he has left off pressing me to marry and settle down. It is a great relief, for you would not credit the lengths he has gone to in order to get me leg-shackled. I would trade the title for such peace any day—though if I could find another like Juliana, I own I might be tempted."

"She is pretty, yes?" Louis asked hopefully. Though he had corresponded with his cousin, he'd not set eyes on her since they were children and it was not the sort of thing one could ask in a letter. "Her papa, my uncle, was considered by many to be a handsome man."

"She is beautiful, Louis. A credit to your family."

A discreet cough caught John's attention and he looked round to see Jenkins standing respectfully a few feet away.

"Beggin' your pardon, my lord, but everything is stowed in the carriage and if you is wishful of reaching Calais tonight, we'd best be on our way."

John nodded. He knew his valet was nervous and the longer they linged in St. Omer, the more worried the poor fellow would be. "I shall be out directly, Jenkins. You may wait for me in the carriage."

"I wish I could persuade you to extend your visit. A week is scarcely long enough to get to know you and, *mon Dieu,* such a week as this! With all the guests and then the military descending upon us, I have had little opportunity to speak with you alone. If only I had known sooner that you meant to visit—"

"My fault," Johnny interrupted. "The visit was a mere impulse—Spencer thought it desirable I absent myself from London for a time and there was Juliana with a letter from you—it seemed fortuitous. I am the one who should apologise for dropping in uninvited."

"No, no, you must not think so. We are relations now and my home is always open to you, but you must promise to visit again when you can stay longer. Perhaps when Juliana comes in October?"

"You are too kind and perhaps something might be contrived, but for now I must take my leave." He held out his hand. "Thank you, Louis, for all your hospitality."

The Frenchman waved aside his hand and hugged him warmly. "Remember, I meant what I said. Should you find yourself in trouble while in France, or have need of assistance, I hope you will trust me to help you. We are *en famille* now."

Johnny felt a twinge of conscience and prayed Louis would never suffer any trouble over this visit. He never should have used Juliana's cousin, but when he'd learned Louis was situated in St. Omer, so close to Calais, it had seemed a heaven-sent opportunity. He'd not expected Louis Chevron to welcome him so effusively, or to like the man so much.

"WILL YOU TRY not to look as though you were climbing the steps to the guillotine," Johnny whispered to Jenkins once their valises and trunks were loaded and the doors of the Custom House had swung safely shut behind them.

"Like as not, that's where we will end up if you continue with this madness," his valet replied tartly. "Did you note the way that officer stared at us? And he searched every bit of our baggage."

"I warned you to expect that," Johnny said, giving leave to the boy to stand away from the horses. He waited until Jenkins swung up beside him. "What was there in that to set you shivering like a wet hen? You knew we had nothing to fear from a search."

"It was like he could see into my head. And there was Lady Throckmorton in front of us. If they had demanded to go through her trunks as they did ours—"

"There was never a chance of that," Johnny said, with a wry grin. "How could you doubt it after spending a week in the same house with her? She's more than a match for any Custom Officer."

"Well, I'm thankful it's over all the same."

"Not quite. We've still the crossing in the morning and then the slight problem of retrieving those papers." The smile disappeared from his lips and his blue eyes took on a glazed look. No matter how smooth the sailing or how calm the Channel might be, he was invariably deathly sick. And if the winds kicked up and the water turned rough, he knew he would spend the next four or five hours feeling not only as though death were imminent but something to be devoutly hoped for.

He tried to put the matter from his mind and deftly drove his carriage into the yard of the Hotel Angleterre. The place was swarming with Englishmen, both arriving and departing. There would be no problem selling the carriage he'd purchased for his brief stay in France.

Johnny left his valet to see to such details and strode into the inn. A babel of noise greeted him, and the sounds of English and French voices raised in heated dispute was enough to make a sane man depart. He paused for a moment, allowing his eyes to adjust to the dim light. Without seeming to, he took note of every person in the room.

It appeared that most of Louis Chevron's guests had arrived before him. He spotted Lady Pennington, Miss Audley, Lord Claypool and Percy Montbalm standing in a small circle near the inner door. He recognised a number of other acquaintances from England but knew a moment's worry when he failed to find any sign of Lady Throckmorton.

Then Miss Talbot stepped into the room and he relaxed, watching her as she moved with single-minded intention through the press of travellers. She stopped to speak to the proprietor and he could only imagine her soft, well-modulated voice. She was the only person in the room who appeared cool and serenely untroubled. Whatever her request, the proprietor nodded agreeably and she turned to make her way back towards the door which led up to the bedchambers. Just for a brief second she glanced about, her lips seeming to curve in a smile of amusement over the rampant confusion.

Her smile was apparently mistaken for one of invitation and a man who had reeled out of the taproom leered at her and stumbled forward to grab her clumsily round the waist. He towered over the lady and tried to plant a kiss on her lips as she struggled to free herself.

Johnny took a step forward but before he could reach Miss Talbot, another Englishman moved in with lightning speed. It was prettily done. One hand gripped the assailant by the collar of his coat and the other his breeches. The drunken sot was hauled off her and sent sprawling on the floor. There were hoots of laughter as the poor fellow looked round, bewildered to find himself in such a position.

Miss Talbot stepped back, gathering her skirts round her, and blushing to find herself the centre of such unwanted attention. Several men called out unflattering advice and the few ladies present delicately looked away.

Johnny stayed where he was, hidden from Miss Talbot's eyes by the half-open door to the dining-room, and cursing beneath his breath at such ill-fated luck. He had recognised the tall, blond-haired gentleman at once. Of all the men to come to the lady's rescue, it would have to be Simon Yorke, the Viscount Brownlow. Johnny hadn't seen him in years, but it didn't appear as if the rogue had changed any, and he edged closer to hear what the viscount might be saying to her.

"My pleasure, my dear Miss Talbot. I am only grateful that I was at hand when you had need of me. These inns have become notoriously ill-bred places and I fear you should not venture belowstairs alone. Will you allow me to escort you back to the hall?"

"Yes, if you would be so good," she murmured, eyes downcast and plainly embarrassed. "I only came down to bespeak dinner for my mother and grandmother."

"You dine in your room, then? That is undoubtedly wise, but I am disappointed not to have the opportunity this evening to better our acquaintance. Tell me, Miss Talbot, are you just arriving in France, or departing for home?"

"We sail for Dover in the morning, sir," she said, pausing at the door to the hall and extending her hand. She raised her eyes to meet his. "I must thank you again for your intervention. It was most kind of you."

"Not at all, dear lady. Any gentleman here would count himself privileged to have done the same."

"You are too modest, sir," she countered, and looking out over the room saw Johnny lounging against the wall a few feet away. He appeared amused, and her back stiffened. When she spoke, her voice carried easily to his ears. "I am acquainted with at least a few gentlemen here, sir, but none with your courage. I consider myself indebted to you."

Simon Yorke bowed and allowed her to go. He had seen the young woman come in with old Lady Throckmorton and thought perhaps the connection could be turned to good advantage. He stared after her, congratulating himself on his unexpected stroke of good fortune. When he turned back to the taproom, he found Johnny blocking his way.

"Turning over a new leaf, Brownlow? I would have thought rescuing damsels in distress a bit out of your line."

"Well, well. If it isn't pretty Lord John. What brings you to France?"

"Nothing that would concern you. Miss Talbot, however, is a friend of mine and I'd not look kindly upon any gentleman who tried to take advantage of her."

"Oh, ho! Did I spoil your sport, perhaps? Did you intend to play the heroic saviour? Too bad, Drayton, but the lady seems to have a liking for my company."

He started to turn away, but Lord John detained him, laying a hand compellingly on his sleeve.

"The lady is an innocent— Oh, but how dreadfully stupid of me. My apologies, Brownlow. I did not mean to rake up that old scandal when you tried to abduct another innocent young lady. Fancy my forgetting that. But then, you've been abroad so many years...."

Brownlow deliberately removed Johnny's hand and, withdrawing a linen handkerchief, wiped delicately at his sleeve. "We all made mistakes in our youth, dear boy. Perhaps you've made some of your own. Yes, I am certain of that. I recollect you always had a tendency to intrude where you were least wanted. I should be most careful, my lord. Such a tendency could prove quite . . . fatal.''

CHAPTER TWO

JOHNNY'S WORST FEARS were confirmed the next morning when he stepped outside the inn with Jenkins. The skies were depressingly grey and a stiff breeze was kicking up. The dampness in the salt air made his skin feel clammy and set his stomach churning.

"They'll have to take us out in one of the rowing boats," Jenkins predicted, watching the whitecaps rolling in. "With the winds blowing offshore, it'll be too rough for the packet to get in the harbour. You watch— those thieving frogs will try to overcharge us, knowing we've no choice."

His words were lost on Johnny. The young lord stood stiffly, staring out at the waves cascading against the rocks, nearly mesmerised by their endless motion. After a moment he turned away, swallowing with difficulty against his rising queasiness.

"Feeling a bit off, my lord?" Jenkins asked, belatedly noting the pallor of his master's face. "A cup of sea water will settle you down quick."

Johnny closed his eyes, muttering through clenched teeth, "Arrange for the boat." However much it went against his inclination, there was no choice. He had to be in Dover when Lady Throckmorton landed. But this was service beyond the call of duty, and he would tell the duke so when he saw him again. And he would tell him there would be no more trips to France. Not until they built a bloody bridge across the Channel.

He kept his head down and his thoughts occupied as he retraced his steps to the inn, and nearly collided with a gentleman as he stepped inside. He drew back, words of apology on his lips, and met the amused eyes of Lieutenant Jennot.

"Thinking of crossing this morning, my lord? If you will pardon my saying so, you look the sort that should wait for calmer seas, unless of course there is some urgency about your business?"

"None, Lieutenant, save a desire for good English food. I fear the crab served last night cannot have been quite fresh. I spent a most restless night. But what of you, sir? Still chasing your spy?"

"I am convinced he is near at hand," the officer said, his eyes narrowing as he carefully watched the young lord's reaction.

"Really?" John asked with studied nonchalance, and looked idly about the room. His gaze fell on Brownlow, standing at the foot of the stairs, bowing over Lady Throckmorton's hand. He lowered his voice and murmured, "You did say the fellow was of my height but with golden curls?"

"So it has been reported," the lieutenant replied, and glanced in the direction his lordship was staring. "Ah, you are thinking of the viscount. We have had him under observation, but it seems Lord Brownlow was rather occupied at the time in question."

"Was he, now? With a lady, perhaps? Someone who might be unduly influenced to swear he was present when in fact he was elsewhere?"

"You surprise me, my lord. I would have wagered you were not the sort to throw suspicion on one of your compatriots."

"Frankly, Lieutenant, I don't care for the fellow, and if directing your attention to him should enrich me by twenty thousand pounds, I should consider the morning well spent."

"Your animosity would not have anything to do with the flattering attention Miss Talbot is bestowing on that gentleman? I should perhaps mention that one of my officers chanced to overhear your conversation with his lordship last evening."

"Which of us were you having followed?" Johnny asked, hoping he appeared to be much amused.

"Lord Brownlow seems to have a way with the ladies," the Frenchman answered, ignoring the question. "Of course, the woman he was with the other evening was not of the same station as Miss Talbot. She was . . . a lady of the evening, so to speak."

"Certainly not the most trustworthy of witnesses, eh, Lieutenant?" Johnny said, and winked lewdly while his stomach continued to churn. "Ah, I see my man and fear you must excuse me, but I hope you will keep Brownlow under observation. If he should prove to be your spy, I intend to return and collect a share of the reward."

"I feel certain you will be . . . present when the reward is paid," the Frenchman replied with a cold bow.

Johnny did not miss the implication, but he met it with a lazy smile and nodded before turning away. He imagined he could feel the eyes of Lieutenant Jennot drilling into his back as he crossed the room. He took Jenkins's arm and urged him out the door. "Have you arranged everything?"

Jenkins nodded. "And none too soon, it 'pears like. You could have knocked me over with a feather when I walked in and saw you with that lieutenant again! I didn't know which way to turn."

"It was something of a surprise to me, as well. However, I've reason to hope I've misdirected his attention to Brownlow, at least momentarily—but Jennot is no fool."

"Then the sooner we set foot on English soil again, the better pleased I'll be. This way, my lord," Jenkins said, indicating the narrow path that led down to the waiting boats.

John tried not to notice how the longboat rocked against the waves, but it was impossible to ignore the water that had splashed inside. There was at least four inches on the bottom and it swirled about his boots as he stepped gingerly aboard. The seats themselves were wet, and within moments the dampness seeped through his trousers. But the discomfort from that was minor compared to the wretched churning of his innards. His stomach heaved violently and he prayed he'd not be sick even before they reached the cutter.

They were the last to board the longboat and the waterman cast off, rowing against the tide and the wind. The boat tilted precariously and Lord John was not the only one to groan at the unsettling motion. He kept his eyes tightly shut while his hands gripped the seat and side of the boat, but even so he could hear the lady behind him retching miserably and his own stomach roiled in sympathy. He cursed silently the events that had landed him in such a position and with impartiality the duke, the Home Secretary, the Prince Regent and even England.

There was a loud thump and Johnny's eyes flew open. They were now alongside the cutter, which at least had the merit of seeming a trifle more stable than the longboat. He was handed up and with Jenkins's arm to guide his unsteady steps, contrived to walk across the deck without disgracing himself.

"It might be better if you were to stay up here, sir. The fresh air would likely do you good."

One look at the choppy, swirling green sea was enough to convince Lord John to the contrary. The bile rising in his throat prevented him from answering, but his desperate gesture sufficed and Jenkins helped him down the narrow stairway to a large room with berths against each wall.

Johnny reeled as the ship pitched alarmingly and he collapsed into a lower berth.

Jenkins hovered beside him. "I saw Lady Throckmorton and them in the boat behind us and that Lord Brownlow was with 'em," he said, hoping to distract his young lord.

Johnny waved an arm in dismissal and turned to face the wall. The room seemed to tilt at an absurd angle that brought his stomach up into his throat. Even closing his eyes did little to restore his sense of balance. At the moment, Lady Throckmorton and all of England could go to perdition for all he cared.

THE CROSSING was an unusually long one, taking nearly six hours to complete. By the time they finally reached Dover, Johnny felt even death would be preferable to another moment spent on the cutter. The room had become crowded as the rough weather drove more and more of the passengers belowdeck to seek shelter, and a more miserable group of people had rarely been assembled. Even sleep had been denied to him, for it was impossible to doze off amidst the groanings and sounds of retching.

Jenkins, whom the rough seas never bothered in the least, came down at last to fetch him, gazing sympathetically at the sorrowful sight his young lord presented. His hair, which had been brushed smoothly back that morning, was now a damp tangle of riotous curls. His coat and shirt were soaked through with sweat, the collar wilted and the jauntily tied cravat a mass of wrinkles. His valet shook his head sadly and was much inclined to linger belowdeck lest someone see his lordship in such a disgraceful condition. He took a great deal of credit for the figure Lord John cut in Society and was much envied by more than one London valet whose own master had a less than admirable figure.

Pride, however, gave way to compassion at the mournful look in his master's eyes. With Lord John walking unsteadily behind him, he shouldered a number of men aside to clear a path to the steps. "Out of the way, now. Here, you, let his lordship through." There were a few muttered curses and ominous stares, but most of those below were too ill to protest and a way was cleared.

Jenkins climbed the stairs first, and upon reaching deck, turned to lend a hand to Lord John. It never ceased to astonish him how a gentleman so intrepid in all other endeavours could turn so squeamish at a bit of a tossing on the sea.

In a matter of moments, they were on solid footing once again and Lord John took a deep breath of air, his eyes carefully avoiding the foaming spray. "Thank you, Jenkins. I shall be better directly."

"You rest here a bit, my lord, and I'll see if I can find Finley and our carriage."

Johnny nodded and leaned against a large trunk that had been set down on the wharf. He was already feeling immensely improved and thought that a hip bath, a change of raiment and one or two hours of sleep would make a new man of him. The thought was a pleasurable one and he hoped Jenkins would be quick with the carriage.

"Well, well! What have we here? Stay a moment, Miss Talbot. The poor wretch looks in need of assistance."

Johnny straightened and turned reluctantly, recognising the syrupy voice of Brownlow behind him. He had Miss Talbot on his arm, and Lady Throckmorton and Mrs. Talbot directly behind him.

"Why, it is Lord John," Brownlow said, feigning surprise, while his dark eyes glittered with undisguised malice. "I vow I would not have recognised you. My dear fellow, you look positively ill."

"I fear I shall never make a sailor," Johnny said and managed a half bow in the direction of the ladies.

"It is simply a matter of will," Lady Throckmorton told him with a marked lack of sympathy. "I've no patience with you fellows who mollycoddle yourselves. If you allow yourself to believe you're going to be sick, then of course you will. Now, if you—"

"Come, Grandmama," Miss Talbot interrupted, feeling a tiny twinge of sympathy for Lord John in spite of herself. "Not everyone has your constitution and the crossing was particularly rough."

"Nonsense. It did not bother Lord Brownlow or you. Violet was the only one who was squeamish, but I dare say that was the strawberries. I warned her last evening how it would be, but then she has never listened to my advice and, as usual, suffers the consequences."

"Yes, Mother," Violet murmured, eyes downcast.

"My brother says it is the same with every generation," Johnny said, hoping to divert her. "I wonder, did you always follow your own mother's advice, Lady Throckmorton?"

"You are an impertinent young man," she retorted, and then nudged Brownlow with her walking stick. "Why are you keeping us standing about? If you proceed in this manner, the rooms will all be taken before we reach the inn. The King's Arms is the only decent hotel in Dover and with that crowd of mushrooms that crossed with us clamouring for rooms, they will be booked full before you can blink."

If Brownlow was embarrassed to be ordered about thusly, he covered it quickly and said smoothly, "You will excuse us, Lord John? I loathe leaving you in such poor straits, but I must think of the ladies. Perhaps I could send someone back from the inn to assist you?"

"You are too kind, Brownlow, but my man will be back directly and I am certain he has already bespoken a room for me." He turned to Lady Throckmorton and bowed. "Pray let me know if you arrive too late to secure accommodations. I would deem it an honour to give up my room for your sake."

"Very pretty," she said, before nudging Brownlow again, and as they moved away remarked to Diana, "at least that brother of his seems to have taught him some manners."

"Indeed," Miss Talbot replied in her cool, clear voice. "Though it would be a pity to turn him from his room. He looks a great deal more in need of it than we."

Johnny heard her plainly, as he suspected he was meant to do. Any pretension that he had scored a point was wiped from his mind and his humiliation was complete when he heard Brownlow's grating laugh floating back to him.

His self-esteem was assuaged a few moments later when Jenkins returned with his groom, Finley, his lordship's own post-chaise and an impressive looking team of high-stepping blacks. Though Finley had protested heatedly at being left to kick his heels at The King's Arms and had seen his lordship depart for France with a scowl of disapproval and dire threats of disaster, he was now all flattering concern.

Lord John was assisted into his carriage with due ceremony and in a matter of moments was passing the walking party of Brownlow and Lady Throckmorton. He hesitated, but did not offer them a ride. It was no great distance to the inn and he'd had time to realise what a disreputable appearance he presented. He was not overly vain, but Miss Talbot had seen him at his worst and her remark still rankled.

The inn was doing a thriving business and Johnny was thankful he'd had the foresight to leave Finley in the room he'd engaged before departing for France. He only hoped Lady Throckmorton would be able to bully the proprietor into providing her with accommodations. He'd whispered quick instructions to his groom and knew he could trust Finley to follow her if she was forced to remove elsewhere. But at present, his greatest concern was for a bath.

Jenkins soon had a hot, scented tub ready for Johnny to step into, and removed his master's offending clothes from sight. He laid out fresh nightclothes for his lordship, turned back the covers on the bed and drew the curtains across the window.

He feared the noise rising from the common rooms and courtyard below would disturb his master, but in spite of his young lord's protest that he'd no need for sleep now, Johnny's head had barely hit the pillow before his eyes closed and he was sound asleep. Jenkins stayed quietly in the room, guarding him from any intrusion, and would not even allow Finley in the chamber, but stepped into the hall for a word with him.

When Johnny awoke a few hours later, Jenkins told him that Lady Throckmorton, by dint of bribing a cit to turn over his room, had secured two bedchambers at the end of the hall. She had the corner room to herself, her daughter and granddaughter the other adjoining it. Lord Brownlow had chanced to meet an old acquaintance staying at the inn and had persuaded him to put him up in his room, so he was here, too.

"Excellent," Johnny said, "though I could do without Brownlow's presence."

"He may be of some use, my lord, if I may be so bold as to say so," Jenkins replied, sharpening his razor in preparation for shaving the unbecoming black stubble from his lordship's face. "Finley tells me he heard Lord Brownlow invite Lady Throckmorton's party to dinner. He's reserved a private sitting room downstairs."

Johnny, his chin swathed in a hot towel, could not answer, but the mischievous light in his eyes was sufficient for Jenkins.

"Yes, my lord, I thought you'd be pleased."

IT WAS CLOSE on seven o'clock when Lord John stepped out of his room that evening, assured by the mirror that he once more looked presentable. That, perhaps, was an understatement. His dark curls had been tamed and brushed smoothly back from the noble brow. A pale blue coat of superfine cloth fitted snugly over his wide shoulders. His cravat, crisply white, was tied in that most difficult of styles, the Oriental. His waistcoat, in an intricate pattern of blue and cream, had been chosen with a discerning eye and went admirably with the biscuit-coloured pantaloons that moulded his long legs. Even his Hessian boots had been restored to a high gloss so the gold tassels adorning them were reflected twice over. And if any were in doubt of the consequence of the gentleman, one had only to note the quizzing glass on a black ribbon about his lordship's neck, the delicate fob at his waist and the elaborately worked snuffbox he carried in his hand.

His nonchalant air proclaimed him the idle, utterly bored gentleman about Town, quite willing to be amused by whatever fancy should catch his interest. But if one looked closely, nothing could quite disguise the intelligence in the blue eyes, or the muscular shape of his thighs and shoulders. The two chambermaids he passed in the hall did not look closely. They were both pleased and embarrassed by his cheerful greeting and flirtatious smile, and huddled together staring after him in an agony of blushes and giggles.

Lord John paused at the door of the taproom, a small smile of amusement at the girls' antics still lingering on his lips. It was crowded, and the noise was well above that level which would allow amiable conversation. He recognised one or two acquaintances from London, but there was no sign of Brownlow and he was about to turn away when Francis Pindar hailed him.

"Johnny, over here," he called, waving enthusiastically from a long table about which clustered half a dozen strangers.

Francis considered himself in debt to Johnny and was embarrassingly effusive whenever he chanced to run across him. He had once been waylaid by a highwayman and returned to London dreadfully shaken by the ordeal. Lord Cochrane, a nasty-tongued coxcomb, had made sport of his terror and poor Francis was the butt of many lewd jokes until Johnny, in his usual madcap way, had taught Cochrane a lesson. He and his friend Somerset had dared to hold up Cochrane's own coach. The little bully had not been so brave when faced with what he thought was a real highwayman.

"Let me stand you a drink," Francis yelled as Lord John made his way through the crowd. "It's the least I owe you."

"What brings you to Dover, Francis? Thinking of going abroad for a bit? I cannot recommend it, just now."

His friend nodded shyly and waved for the serving wench. She came promptly, her round eyes raking greedily over Lord John and her lips curving in an inviting smile. She pressed against him deliberately, her heavy perfume enveloping them.

Johnny grinned down at her, deftly plucking a mug of ale from her serving tray.

"I hear the Domino has struck again," Francis was saying, while he admired the easy way Johnny had with the lasses. "Everyone's been talking about it and the way the Frenchies are searching every Englishman. Is it true, John, that they've posted a twenty-thousand-pound reward on his head?"

"So I have heard," Johnny answered, winking at the serving wench as she walked away. Her wide hips swayed enticingly as she smiled at him over her shoulder.

"Well, I hardly need worry. No one would suspect me of masquerading as the Black Domino, that much is for certain."

"They'll suspect anyone speaking the King's English, Francis. Unless your visit is of urgency, I suggest you wait a bit to see Paris."

"But you've just come back, and I saw Lord Brownlow—"

"When?" Johnny interrupted more forcefully than he intended. "I wanted a word with him," he explained, and then added more casually, "Is he somewhere about?"

"He was here a few moments ago," Francis said, peering vaguely round. "He said something about arranging a card game later. I confess I was flattered to be asked."

"Take my advice and save your shillings. Join me for a drink this evening instead," Johnny said, and took a heavy swallow of ale. "Brownlow must be in need of funds if he's setting up a game so soon, and no doubt looking for a lamb in need of fleecing."

"Well, I fancy I can hold my own with the best of them when it comes to cards," Francis said, a trifle miffed that his friend would think him a green one.

"I've no doubt of it—if the game is an honest one," Johnny replied quietly, leaning close to Francis under the pretext of setting down his glass.

"Johnny! You are not suggesting Brownlow would cheat—"

"Let us say only that I think you would find my company preferable. Now, don't stir up any trouble, Francis. Leave that to the French. I've a few things to attend to, but I shall look to see you later."

Johnny clasped him on the shoulder and then made his way through the room. He hoped his warning to Francis wouldn't reach Brownlow's ears. A duel at present would be dashed inconvenient. He should have been more discreet, of course, but Pindar was just the sort of easy mark a shark like Brownlow would prey on.

He sidestepped a gentleman who'd had a bit much to drink and looked in the door of the dining-room. It was early yet and only a few of the travellers had sat down to eat. There were at least two private sitting-rooms and

Johnny went along the hall to the nearest and lounged by the door. There were no sounds from within and he risked easing the door open for a look. The table was laid for four, but the room was as yet unoccupied. He shut the door again and strolled nonchalantly towards the other room. It was situated well at the back of the inn and he wondered what excuse he'd give if Brownlow chanced to find him there.

The door opened abruptly and Lieutenant Jennot stepped out. "Looking for someone, Lord John?" he asked, drawing the door tightly shut behind him and leaning against it.

"Lady Throckmorton," he said, grinning. At least that had the merit of being true. "I fear Brownlow stole a march on me and has invited the ladies to be his guests for dinner this evening."

"Then he must have engaged the other sitting-room," the lieutenant said, and nodded towards the hall. "I bespoke this room for myself and my men—unless, of course, you would care to join us?"

"You are too kind, Lieutenant, but another time, perhaps?"

"Certainly, my lord, I expect we shall have occasion to meet again before long."

"I shall look forward to it," Johnny murmured as he hastily retreated. The blasted lieutenant seemed to be everywhere. He heard the sound of a door shutting softly and risked a glance back. Jennot was no longer in sight but that singular fact failed to reassure him, and he thought the sooner he swept the dust of Dover from his boots the better it would be. He swung round the corner and heard Lady Throckmorton's strident tones.

He stepped quickly back and prayed Lieutenant Jennot would remain safely in his sitting-room.

"Whatever they serve, it is certain to be an improvement over French cuisine. If you ask me, it is all pretension and I deplore the way certain people feel compelled to rave over food I would not consider fit to serve my dogs."

"Now, Mother, a few of the dishes we were served had some merit. The creamed asparagus over—"

"There! That is precisely what I meant," Lady Throckmorton interrupted her daughter. "You are just like the rest of them, and fear to be thought provincial if you don't find some dish or other to exclaim over. You agree with me, don't you, Brownlow?"

"I fear I am a poor judge, my lady. After a year abroad my palate has become jaded though I confess I am eager for the taste of good English food. I missed it quite dreadfully."

"Well, I do not agree," Diana said.

Johnny heard the sound of her appealing laugh, which for some reason or other always reminded him of the sun coming out after a heavy storm, and he could not help smiling.

"As for your dogs, Grandmama, they are excessively spoiled and eat better than most people, and if you were not so stubborn you would admit that Mama is in the right of it. I enjoyed quite a number of dishes and I believe one must approach foreign food as a new experience. One cannot after all expect the French to cook as we do, and if they did what would be the point in travelling abroad at all?"

"There was no point in it, miss, not with you behaving the way you did, and had I known how it would be, I would never have set foot outside England. A shameless waste of time and money to be traipsing all over the

Continent to provide you with opportunities you choose to ignore. Well, my girl, I warn you that is all at an end."

Johnny, shamelessly eavesdropping now, would have given much to hear Diana's answer, but the door to the sitting-room closed firmly on the party. He could hear the murmur of their voices, but could not distinguish any words. He waited another moment to be certain they were settled and then strolled leisurely down the hall. He gave the taproom and common rooms a wide berth and made for the stairs.

He encountered several gentlemen just coming down and nodded pleasantly. It appeared every one of the inn's guests was preparing to dine, and the upper hall was deserted and strangely quiet after the din below. This would surely be the best opportunity he'd have to retrieve his papers. The ladies should be occupied for some time.

Miss Talbot's bedchamber lay on the opposite side of the inn. He found the room with ease, and making short work of the lock, was inside in a matter of seconds. Johnny stood with his back against the door, barely breathing, and every sense alert for an unexpected presence. He relaxed after a moment, hardly surprised to find the room deserted. One of the reasons he'd chosen Miss Talbot to transport the papers was his knowledge of Lady Throckmorton's parsimony, which led her to travel without servants. Precaution was second nature to him however, and it was due to such measures that he'd thus far escaped detection.

Now, with cat-like stealth, he moved across the room to where the baggage had been hastily stowed. Lady Throckmorton planned to leave in the morning and Miss Talbot had wisely not bothered with unpacking anything but the essentials she needed for the evening. He had counted on that. The hatbox he'd chosen stood on top of a heavy trunk, the elaborately worked design marking it a creation of Paris.

Johnny carefully lifted out the fetching concoction of straw adorned with numerous ostrich feathers dyed a pale blue and entwined with blue silk ribbons. He studied it as he held it up, imagining how delightful Miss Talbot would look in it, and then laid it aside. The bottom of the box was stuffed with newspapers to help retain the shape of the hat and it was beneath these that he had secreted his hooded black domino and the oilskin-wrapped packet of papers.

He drew it forth, shaking out the folds of the silk cape to make certain the papers were safe. Everything appeared to be in order, and he was hastily stuffing the newspaper back in the box when his keen ears caught the sound of light footsteps in the hall. He lifted his head, intently listening, and cursed lightly beneath his breath as the steps continued in his direction.

One glance at the grime-encrusted window was sufficient to assure him that it offered no hope of escape. The papers were shoved beneath his waistcoat even as he heard the rattle of a key. He had just enough time to settle the hooded cape over his head and adjust his mask before the door swung open.

CHAPTER THREE

DIANA TALBOT STOOD just inside the doorway, the light from the hall illuminating her. She remained perfectly still, fearful the gentleman would disappear in a puff of smoke were she to move suddenly. A black hood covered his hair and fell in silk swirls to his boots. A half mask, tied at either side of the hood, effectively covered his eyes and nose. But she did not need to see his features to know this man. He had been in her dreams countless nights.

Johnny had time to admire the long, flowing lines of her ivory satin gown and to note how snugly it fit about the bosom. The neck was cut low in the new style, but was offset with delicate, hand-woven black roses that rested against her creamy skin. A single strand of pearls encircled her slender throat and matching earrings decorated the delicate lobes of her ears, though they were nearly hidden by wisps of curls that appeared to have escaped from her elaborate coiffure.

Johnny thought, quite irrelevantly, that her hair seemed to gleam like copper in the dim light. He had always preferred women with silky black tresses, but at the moment, he would have given much to unloosen the pins holding Miss Talbot's long chestnut curls and watch them cascade down about her pretty shoulders and over her very enticing bosom.

For a brief instant they continued to stare at each other.

Diana moved first, reaching behind her to close the door, shutting out the light. The room was now dimly lit by the one taper on the bedside table, and silent save for the soft swirl of her gown.

He watched her, his dark brows arching at her impudence. This was not the way a well-bred young lady should react to finding a masked man in her room. She should either swoon or retreat screaming into the hall, but he was not really surprised that she chose to do neither. He smiled and made her a sweeping bow.

"Your pardon, Miss Talbot, for the intrusion. I had thought you to be dining below."

"You know me, sir?" she asked, a breathlessness disturbing her normal cool tones.

"Not as well as I should like to, my dear," he replied huskily, keeping his voice pitched low while his eyes watched her every move, but she seemed unafraid and even dared to take a step or two closer.

"Or I," she replied softly. It was incredibly bold of her, and a tinge of colour flushed her cheeks, but she found it inconceivable that she should be expected to behave with missish propriety when the hero of her dreams had suddenly appeared in her room. Surely, she thought, one could be forgiven for dispensing with the tenets of polite behaviour on such an occasion, and dared to take a step closer to him.

"You know me better than you think, Miss Talbot, but for the sake of us both, I can say no more." He cursed his tongue as soon as the words were said. Gad, he sounded like some glib paper hero from a penny novel and would not have been much astonished had she laughed aloud.

Miss Talbot, however, apparently saw nothing amiss with his choice of dialogue. Her brown eyes were glowing with an unnatural brilliance and her soft lips opened slightly. She reached out a hand impulsively. "Pray, do not say another word if you think it unwise. Not for the world would I endanger you. But how came you to be here? Do you not realise the hotel is full of French officers, and they are all searching for you?"

He nodded, making a supreme effort to keep his eyes off the delectable cut of her gown's neckline. Her embroidered shawl had slipped off her shoulders and the rise and fall of her breasts was having a disastrous effect on his wits. With an effort, he brought his gaze up to her face and tried to concentrate on what she was saying.

"The lieutenant told us there is a reward of twenty thousand pounds for information laid against you. Is it not dangerous for you to be here? There are those below who would betray you without a second thought for half such a fortune."

Her voice was husky with concern and Johnny saw the worry reflected in her eyes. He stepped closer and whispered, "But am I not safe with you? You would not betray me, would you, my dear? Even for so prodigious an amount?"

"Not for any sum," she said, looking up at him, the words a sworn oath. He was so close now that she could feel his warm breath on her cheeks, and still it was not enough. In her dreams, he had held her tightly in his arms and she yearned for him to do so now.

Johnny read the invitation in her eyes and captured her hands in his own, as much to steady himself as her. "Thank you for that, sweetheart, though I was already certain I could trust you. In truth, I had little choice. The lieutenant has been hard on my heels this trip and I was compelled to hide the papers he searches for so assiduously. I knew even if you found them, you would not hand them over to the French."

"If I found them—but where?" she asked in some confusion.

He pointed in the direction of her hatbox. "They were smuggled ashore beneath your very fetching hat, and right past Lieutenant Jennot's long nose."

"But how ever did you manage it? I had no notion—"

"Oh, it was easy enough at the inn in Calais," he said, regretting the lie but knowing it would be beyond foolish to mention the house in St. Omer. For now at least, his identity must be kept secret. "You must not think you were in danger," he added, anxious to change the subject. "I was near at hand and if the papers had been discovered, I would have stepped forward at once."

"And been hanged for your chivalry," she cried, horrified at the thought.

"Better I than you, my dear."

"No, oh, no. England could easily spare a dozen like me, but there is only one Black Domino."

"And blasphemous to suggest there are dozens like you," he replied gallantly, his voice low with passion. Unable to resist, he released her hands and drew her close. One hand caressed her cheek while the other encircled her waist. "I have never met another... not with brown eyes so lustrous or skin as soft as a rose...." he said, bending his head to brush her lips.

Diana knew she should draw away but it was impossible to do so. She had dreamed of this moment a thousand times. She shut her eyes, blocking out the dreary room and allowed her arms to creep up about his neck. Her mouth opened to receive his kisses, but nothing in her dreams had prepared her for the rush of passion that flooded her body. The feeling was intoxicating and she wanted it never to end.

Johnny was startled at the warmth of her response. He had kept a succession of mistresses, but not one of them had ever kissed him with such pure, unbridled enjoyment. His arms tightened about her. He could feel the buttons and tiny hooks that lined the back of her gown. For a moment he was tempted to undo it, but he drew back and looked down at Diana. Her eyes fluttered open, hazy with desire.

"I never knew...a kiss could make one feel quite so...so wonderful," she murmured.

"It doesn't always," he said, and kissed the tip of her nose before setting her firmly away from him. One of them had to think clearly. He brushed a curl away from her cheek. "Is anyone likely to come looking for you?"

"Oh, heavens! Grandmama! I forgot—she sent me up to fetch a clean handkerchief for her. They will be wondering what has become of me."

"Tell her you had trouble finding one in the trunk. Everything is still packed," Johnny advised. "But you must hurry back. I was surprised you returned here alone. What is the old lady about to let you go round unescorted?"

"Oh, we are just in the sitting-room at the foot of the steps," she said, lifting the heavy lid of the chest and searching through the pile of linen.

"It is still dangerous for you to be wandering about the halls alone. I would not allow it, had I the right."

Her eyes told him she would willingly grant him that right—and any others he chose to accept. Johnny drew in a sharp breath. "You had best return before Lady Throckmorton becomes alarmed. Hurry down and I will stay here with the door ajar. You have only to shout if you have need of me.''

She allowed him to escort her to the door, reveling in the firm touch of his hand on her back, but she hesitated there and turned to face him. ''Will I ever see you again?''

''Beyond a doubt, and much sooner than you might think,'' he said, imagining her surprise when he revealed his identity. He had to stifle a laugh as he thought of her certain disbelief, and searched his mind for some sure way to convince her. His eyes fell on the intricate hand-worked black roses that adorned the scalloped neck of her gown. His reached up and with a slender finger gently traced the edge of her bodice. ''When this business is done, I shall come to you openly and you will know me by the black rose I carry in memory of this night.''

She did not flinch from his touch, and Johnny was close enough to feel her quickened breath and see the excitement flare in her eyes.

''I think that I should always recognise you, no matter your disguise,'' she said, half-wishing she could push the hooded cloak away from his hair, and untie the strings of the mask. Still, his words had given her a hint and she added softly, ''I am certain I already know your identity, my lord.''

He touched her lips with his fingers to halt her words. ''Do not even attempt to guess,'' he warned. ''It is far safer for you not to know.''

''Perhaps, but I fear you are the one who is in grave danger, and I shall pray for your safety until we meet again,'' she whispered, her hand on the door.

''Go quickly, my dear,'' he said, no longer trusting himself to be alone with her. Her words had filled him with such a surge of energy that he feared he might do something reckless. His chest expanded, the blood dancing through his veins. He could easily pick her up and crush her to him in his exuberance.

"And you? How will you leave?" she asked, delaying the moment when they must part.

He stepped backwards, knowing he needed distance between them before he yielded to baser impulses. This was no time for dalliance. Lives were at risk. He knew it and yet still had to suppress an insane boyish urge to throw his cape across his shoulder and leap from the window in a final, impressive gesture.

He confined his madness to edging towards the window, but could not resist a last sweeping bow and blew a kiss to her from the tips of his fingers. "Go, my fair Diana, and never look back."

She tried to obey him and had turned from the door, but could not control the impulse for one last glimpse of him. She paused, tilted her head and lifted a delicate hand in salute before walking slowly down the hall.

Diana floated down the stairs, full of the heady knowledge that she had only to lift her voice and he would come to her, no matter the danger to himself. Of course she would not do so. Not even when two gentlemen, much the worse for drink, made lewd suggestions as they passed. Diana ignored them, barely hearing their words and entered the sitting-room with scant awareness of how she had arrived there. Her mother and grandmother were waiting for her, the latter with every indication of impatience.

"What took you so long, miss? I was about to send Violet in search of you. Well? Don't stand there looking like a moonling! Sit down, for heaven's sake."

Diana took her seat feeling as though she had just awakened from a dream, and wishing very much that she could drift back to sleep. Her grandmother's sharp voice precluded that, however, and she handed over the lace-edged handkerchief.

"This is not mine—it's one of Violet's," Lady Throckmorton said in lieu of any thanks, and looked at the offending square of linen as though it were in some way repulsive.

"I am sorry, Grandmama. Everything is packed away and I had some trouble finding even that one."

"It's all of a piece. First Brownlow disappears and then you. In my day, things were done differently. A gentleman did not leave ladies alone in an hotel room where anyone could intrude on their privacy. If I had known he meant to desert us in such a shabby manner, I would have ordered dinner in our rooms."

"Now, Mother, you know Lord Brownlow explained his business was urgent. I am sure he will return in a very few minutes."

Diana looked down at her cooling soup, not at all surprised that the viscount was still absent, and thought she knew what urgent business he was about. The Domino, though perhaps he'd not realised it, had given her several clues to his identity.

"Diana! I have spoken to you twice. Are you ill, girl?"

"No, Grandmama. I beg your pardon. I was just…just thinking." Thinking and remembering the feel of his lips on hers. Her finger traced the line of her mouth in an effort to retrace the rapture she'd felt.

"Daydreaming again! It is enough to put one out of patience with you. When we return to London—" She broke off abruptly as the door opened and Brownlow entered.

He was full of profuse apologies for his delayed absence. It had, regrettably, been necessary, but Lady

Throckmorton appeared unimpressed and it was Diana who spoke up in his defence.

"You are too hard on the gentleman, Grandmama," she said with a small laugh, and turned to smile warmly up at him. "I am so glad you are safely returned, my lord."

Her grandmother raised her quizzing glass and peered across the table and still could hardly credit her eyes. Her granddaughter was actually blushing and was speaking to the viscount as though he were a favoured suitor. The words were simple enough, but the tone! Perhaps there was hope for the girl, after all.

Mrs. Talbot, though not especially observant, was equally surprised. Diana had shown Lord Brownlow nothing but a common civility, and accorded him only the barest courtesies. There had been no hint in her manner to allow her mother, whatever her hopes, to suppose anything would come of the chance acquaintance.

Even Brownlow was put a little off balance by the warmth in Diana's eyes, but he was ever ready to take advantage of any opportunity and he smiled at her. "Thank you, Miss Talbot. I am distressed to think my absence caused you the least concern, but confess I consider myself fortunate to be in your thoughts at all, whatever the reason."

"Well, don't go giving yourself airs. She cannot have missed you that much," Lady Throckmorton snapped. "Diana only just returned before you did and why it should take her above a quarter hour to find a handkerchief is beyond me."

Diana, feeling unaccountably disappointed at the viscount's glib reply, spoke more sharply than she intended. "I explained what happened, Grandmama."

"Not sufficiently," the old lady said, watching her closely. "I distinctly recall placing a dozen clean handkerchiefs at the top of my valise. You must be going blind to have missed them."

"I missed them because I did not enter your room," Diana said and realised too late her error. She made an effort to recover. "I thought I heard a noise in our room—but it was nothing. The wind perhaps."

Mrs. Talbot made a valiant effort to redirect the conversation, enquiring of Lord Brownlow if he had patronised The King's Arms before.

Lady Throckmorton allowed her daughter to ramble on and barely paid heed to the viscount's reply. Something was afoot, of that she was certain. Diana was behaving strangely and as she tried to puzzle out what could have occurred to discompose the girl, an absurd thought entered her head. She paused, her fork in mid-air and stared at her granddaughter.

Diana, sensing her regard, glanced at her. "Is something amiss, Grandmama?" It took an effort, but her voice was calm and she met her grandmother's gaze serenely.

"Nothing," Lady Throckmorton said, convinced she must be wrong. She laid down her fork. "Brownlow, this chicken is overdone and dry as the bone. Ring for the girl and have it removed, if you please. I shall try some of the fish."

She sipped at her wine while the covers were changed, keeping a sharp eye on the others. Brownlow's manner towards Diana had not changed at all. Nor could she detect the slightest sign in her granddaughter now that she regarded him more warmly than she had before. Which was to say, not at all.

Lady Throckmorton withdrew from the conversation. She ate little but continued to drink the wine and by the third glass was nearly convinced she'd been wrong. She supposed it was ludicrous to think her very proper and reserved granddaughter would meet secretly with the viscount. It was the sort of thing *she* might have done when she was Diana's age, but not the girl. Too staid by half. And there was no reason for a tryst. The chit must know such a match would be welcome. Brownlow came from a fine family. She had gone to school with his grandmother. . . .

"Mother?" Violet nudged her softly. "Mother, his lordship wishes to know if you care for dessert."

She shook her head. Lord, the room was stuffy. Another few minutes and she'd be nodding at the table like Lady Cathcart. She rose shakily. "I believe it is time we retired. We must be abroad early."

The viscount was on his feet at once and came round to assist her, pulling out her chair and giving her his arm.

"Thank you, Brownlow. It was a pleasant enough dinner. If you are returning to Town on the morrow, you might care to give us your escort. We leave at half past ten."

"I should be delighted," he said, and had no need to feign enthusiasm. It was what he'd been angling for. The old lady would pay the post charges and he'd save a pretty penny. He shortened his steps to match her small stride and walked with her to the door.

"See you are on time, then," she ordered. "Come along, Violet, Diana."

Mrs. Talbot gave him her hand. "Thank you, my lord for an excellent dinner. So much more enjoyable than being served in one's room. I shall look forward to seeing you on the morrow."

He bowed over her hand politely before turning to Diana.

Feeling safe for the moment from her grandmother's prying eyes, she smiled tenderly up at him, her brown eyes glowing, and whispered breathlessly, "I shall never forget this evening, my lord."

"Nor I, my dear," he returned, swiftly covering his surprise. He leaned over to gently press a kiss on her wrist, just above her glove. Perhaps it was not going to be as difficult as he'd supposed to win over Miss Talbot.

"Diana! Come along, girl!"

"I must go," she said, reluctantly withdrawing her hand. She wondered his touch did not stir her as it had earlier, but assumed it was the knowledge that her grandmother waited a step or two away.

WHILE DIANA WAS DINING, Lord John was losing steadily—much to the delight of Francis Pindar and the two young brothers from Leicester. He knew he was playing carelessly, but he found it impossible to concentrate on the cards. It was his own fault, of course. Although the taproom was a natural place to set up a friendly game, he should never have chosen a table near the door. The slightest noise from the hall brought his head up, anxious to catch a glimpse of Miss Talbot as she stepped out of the sitting-room. He hoped the lady was finding it as difficult to concentrate on polite conversation as he was on the game.

Francis crowed as he swept another hand and Johnny threw in his cards. He wondered that he had never noticed what an annoying laugh that young man had.

"You've Lady Luck sitting on your shoulder tonight," Richard Elmhurst said, throwing down his own cards in disgust. "What say you to another round of ale?"

"Francis can stand us to drinks," Johnny agreed, pushing his empty tankard across the table.

"My pleasure," Pindar chortled, motioning to the serving maid. "I did warn you, John, that I am devilish lucky at cards." He leaned back in his chair, stretching a little and allowing his gaze to travel about the room. "I am glad you suggested we play in here. This is jolly good—all the comforts of the club."

Johnny didn't answer. His attention was riveted on the door. He saw Lady Throckmorton and her daughter come out of the sitting-room, but not Diana. He leaned backward, tilting his chair at a precarious angle, for a better look. He could just make out the sweeping skirt of her gown as she stood in the doorway speaking to Brownlow.

What the devil could she be finding to say to him? He'd have thought that after the tender scene in her room, she would be too occupied with thoughts of the Domino to give Brownlow the time of day.

Even above the near-deafening din of the taproom, he heard Lady Throckmorton's imperious summons. Diana appeared after a moment, but Johnny was hardly reassured. He saw her start towards the steps, trailing after her relatives. Then she paused, turning back to wave at Brownlow. Johnny couldn't see her features clearly, but her stance, the tilt of her head and the graceful wave of her hand seemed to contain an air of intimacy that annoyed him out of reason.

Brownlow stepped into the hall, blocking his vision, and Johnny let his chair crash down. A frown marred his forehead and his eyes darkened ominously as he upended his tankard.

"I say, John, your pockets aren't to let, are they?" Francis asked, a trifle concerned. "You know I would gladly take a vowel from you. No need to pay me now if it leaves you short."

"We shall see who is short when the game is done," Johnny replied, his voice unusually curt. "Deal the cards."

No one said a word for several moments and the hand was played swiftly. The table stakes went to Lord John, but he still looked less than pleased. The deal passed to David Elmhurst, and he shuffled and dealt the cards uneasily.

All four men looked up as a shadow fell across the table.

"Ah, there you are, Pindar," Brownlow said, coming to stand between him and Richard Elmhurst. "I was wondering where you'd disappeared to."

Pindar's face flushed and he stuttered slightly. "I—I did try to find you but you'd gone and, well, Lord John proposed we have a game in here—just penny stakes, you know."

"A trifle tame, is it not? I have arranged for a real game out in the stables."

With the other asses, Johnny thought, but did not say the words. He looked coolly up at Brownlow and the distaste in his eyes was so marked the others sat silent. "Then pray do not allow us to detain you," he said, picking up his cards without looking. He kept his gaze locked on the viscount's eyes.

"Well, it seems I have a bit of a problem, now," Brownlow said, shifting his glance to Francis. "I do wish you had let me know earlier, Pindar, that you did not intend to play. We need a fourth and 'tis a little late to find someone else."

"Pity," Johnny said before Francis could reply. "But I am sure you will find some poor fool."

"How am I to take that?" Brownlow demanded, his fingers curling into a fist.

"Why, as I intended it, of course. Anyone who would prefer to play cards in a drafty stable, amidst a bunch of smelly cattle, must be something of a fool."

"We are playing in the stables because the stakes will be rather high, and we don't want every buffoon in here breathing down our necks!"

"Yes, it is quite annoying to have someone standing behind you when you are trying to concentrate on the cards," Johnny said pointedly. "Do you open, Richard?"

Brownlow hesitated. Had it been anyone else at the table, he would have thrown down a challenge. Lord John, however, was too well known for his skill with both pistols and swords. He swallowed his wrath and stepped to the side, a little closer to Pindar.

"It looks as though your luck is in tonight, Francis. When you are done here, you might still wish to join us."

"Thank you, my lord, but I wouldn't count on it," Pindar replied absently, throwing out the ace of spades. It was well for his peace of mind that he didn't notice the anger that flashed in Brownlow's eyes.

Johnny took the hand easily and Francis groaned. "Drat, I knew I shouldn't lead with spades."

"It was most unfair of us to play while you were engaged," Johnny said. "We should have held up the game until you were done with your conversation. We will wait, if you like. You do not object, do you, gentlemen?"

The Elmhurst brothers agreed it would only be fair.

Francis protested. "No, no. We're done now, I think."
He turned, looking up at Brownlow. "There wasn't anything else, was there, my lord?"

The viscount had little choice. He nodded stiffly and
strolled towards the bar. Johnny noted him leaving an
hour later with a young gentleman who barely looked out
of leading-strings. *Another pigeon,* he thought. Well, he
couldn't rescue them all, though the notion of challeng-
ing Brownlow to a duel had a definite attraction. It was
a pity that he couldn't risk it until the papers were safely
delivered.

JOHNNY STEPPED OUTSIDE the inn and drew in a deep
breath of the cool evening air. Morning air, he amended,
glancing at his fob. It was close to four o'clock and already the sky was beginning to lighten. A yawn escaped
him and he stretched a little, arching his back. The game
had seemed endless, and at any other time he would have
called it quits hours before. Only his determination to
keep Francis from joining Brownlow had kept him in his
seat. That, and the need to win back the fifty pounds he'd
lost earlier. Fancy, letting a female spoil his concentra-
tion.

He glanced up, knowing the room near the corner of
the building was Miss Talbot's. Her window was dark,
the curtains drawn, and he imagined she must be fast
asleep. Unbidden, an image came to mind. He envisaged
her in bed, her eyes shut and her long lashes resting softly
against the curve of her cheek. Her lips were open just
slightly and tendrils of her long chestnut hair lay tangled
about her shoulders. Did she dream of the Black Domino?

"You are abroad rather late, my lord," Lieutenant Jennot said, appearing abruptly from a clump of bushes near the door.

"As are you, Lieutenant. Do you make it a habit to skulk about in the shrubbery?"

"If the occasion warrants it," the officer said, undisturbed. He took out a cigar and lit it, his eyes intent on Lord John.

"I suppose it would be rather futile to suggest this occasion does not."

"Quite, my lord."

"Then I shall leave you to lurk in peace," Johnny said, smothering another yawn. "If it rests your mind, I am for bed and have no intention of stirring before morning."

"You relieve me, sir. I wish you a good night."

"Thank you, Lieutenant. I am certain I shall sleep well knowing you are without, guarding us all."

Johnny left him standing near the shrubbery and strolled back inside. He was wide awake now and pleased that he'd not attempted to pass the papers along the regular courier route. Lieutenant Jennot was most determined. He whistled softly as he made his way up the dimly lit stairs. Jenkins was waiting for him.

"It was just like you thought, my lord. About two o'clock or so, I heard this noise at the door. A scratching like. I coughed just like you said and whoever it was went away. You think it was the Frenchie?"

"I am very nearly certain of it. Had the room been empty or you sound asleep, he would have made a thorough search in here."

"Mayhap we should have left him to it. Then when he found nothing, he might have thought he was wrong."

"I fear it will take more than that to persuade the man," Johnny said, and turned so his valet could remove the tight-fitting coat. The waistcoat and shirt followed, but Johnny refused to allow Jenkins to undo the pouch strapped closely to his chest. He intended to keep the papers close by him until he could deliver them personally to the Duke of Cardiff—a feat that was likely to challenge his ingenuity.

"You think the Frenchie will follow us tomorrow?" Jenkins asked, making an effort to sound unconcerned as he neatly folded his master's shirt and stock.

"More than likely. His only chance now at recovering the papers is to hold us up tomorrow. Somewhere between here and London . . . probably north of Allington."

"He wouldn't dare! Why that's a hanging offence! He'd swing for certain if he was caught."

"So is spying," Johnny said, grinning at the dismay on Jenkins's face. "Apparently the good lieutenant has his orders to recover these papers at all costs."

"What are we to do, then?"

The candle flickered and Jenkins thought it must be a trick of the light that made his master look so suddenly reckless. He stirred uneasily when Johnny threw back his head and laughed aloud.

The room was unduly warm but Jenkins shivered at the sound.

CHAPTER FOUR

LORD JOHN STIRRED in his sleep, disturbed by a commotion in the hall outside his door. He tried ignoring it, pulling a pillow over his head, but the landlord's bellow penetrated even that.

"I'll not be having a wench in the house what's rude to her betters. You been warned before, Poppy Beresford! Now pack your things up and get out!"

The sound of a girl sobbing reached his ears, but her words were lost to him as the landlord castigated her for an idle good-for-nothing who didn't know her place. Johnny sat up and with one fluid movement picked up a boot from beside the bed and hurled it with unerring accuracy at the door. It made a satisfying thud and for a moment there was silence in the hall. Then, hearing the sound of heavy shoes retreating, he prepared to go back to sleep.

He settled down beneath the comfortable, snug quilt, prepared to recapture the pleasant dream he'd been enjoying. A moment later he sighed and reluctantly opened his eyes. Choking sobs, as annoying and intrusive as a leaking ceiling, could be clearly heard. The girl must be right outside his door. He hardly needed to glance round the room to know Jenkins was not there. His valet would never allow anyone to disturb him so early, but where *was* the dratted fellow when he was needed? Grumbling to himself, Johnny climbed out of bed.

He ran a hand through his tousled hair and pulled on his brocade dressing-gown before stumbling to the door. He yanked it open, but whatever words of reproof he intended to utter died on his lips. The child, and it was obvious the girl was still of tender years, sat huddled against the wall opposite. Her knees were drawn up beneath her dingy grey muslin dress, and her skinny arms were wrapped tight about them. Her blond head was bowed and hidden against her skirt, but Johnny could see her shoulders shaking as the child sobbed. His anger evaporated.

"Here now, it cannot be as bad as all that," he said, trying to sound cheerful as he took a step towards her.

The girl looked up. He had a fleeting impression of enormous blue eyes and tear-stained cheeks before she flung her apron over her head and cowered against the wall as though he meant to strike her. He cursed silently but made no further move to reach her. Leaning against the open door of his room, he waited patiently, and after a moment she peeped up at him.

"I mean you no harm, lass, but I cannot very well help you if you will not tell me what is wrong. And I think it's the least you can do after waking me up, you know."

She sniffed quite audibly and swiped at her nose with the sleeve of her dress. It did little to improve her appearance.

"I'm sorry, my lord. I never meant to wake you."

"No, of course you didn't, but what has happened? Did the cliffs fall while I was sleeping and strand us here or has that madman Napoleon escaped yet again and surrounded us?"

She stared up at him, her eyes round with surprise though she little understood his humour, and solemnly shook her head.

"Then what is it, child? Come now, I think you will feel better if you confide in me. Can you stand up? Shall I help you?"

Her shoulders hunched forward and she scrambled to her feet, keeping a wary eye on Lord John as though he might attack her, but he remained lounging against his door, and somewhat reassured, she faced him. "I been turned off," she began softly. "But it ain't no worry of yours and I'm sorry I woke you. It's just I needed the money to help Ma and he owes me for the quarter but now I won't get nothing and..." The words trailed off as she bit her lip in an effort to stem her sobs, but her shoulders were shaking again as she turned away.

"Wait," Johnny called and stepped forward. "Do you know who I am? No, I thought not. Well, in London they call me Saint John, the sworn avenger of chambermaids and serving girls. If you've been treated shabbily, you are supposed to report it to me."

The child hesitated, looking at him curiously. "I ain't never heard of no one like that," she said doubtfully.

"No? Well, that's because you're in Dover and not London. Now what happened, child? Why were you turned off? I heard our good landlord say you were rude to a guest. Is that true?"

She shook her head, blond curls bobbing. "No, sir. Leastways, not like what I think you mean. 'Tis only that one of the gentlemen wanted me to..." Her round little face flamed red and she hung her head, mumbling, "I'm a good girl, my lord, and I don't hold with going to a gentleman's room no matter how much he might be willing to pay."

"I see. And quite right, too. Did some gentleman try to force you to go to his room?"

She nodded, ashamed. "He wouldn't listen and when he grabbed me, I—I kicked him, sir, and ran away. He told Mr. Tibbs this morning that I was rude but it weren't like what he said," she said, sniffing. "And Mr. Tibbs said I weren't no good to him and turned me off and I ain't got no place—"

"Yes, I know. You haven't anywhere to go. Where does your family live?" Johnny asked, thinking that he could at least see the child had stagecoach fare to return safely home.

"In Maldon, sir, but I can't go home," she said, the words ending in a near wail.

"Don't start sobbing again, I beg you," Johnny said. He never could bear the sight of anyone crying. "Tell me why you can't go home. If it's just the fare, I can lend you that."

The girl shook her head but she dried her eyes and between tearful sniffs Johnny finally got the story out of her. Her mother was apparently sickly and doing what she could to support four more youngsters. Poppy, as this absurd child was called, was, at sixteen, the eldest. Her mother was depending on her to help support them. The quarter was almost up and Poppy was due her wages, half of which she was to send home. Only now, of course, she'd not receive a penny.

Johnny considered the matter. The child was not bad-looking, or at least she wouldn't be when her face wasn't splotched with tears and she got some meat on her bones. Obviously, she'd had a decent, moral upbringing. But even if Mr. Tibbs could be persuaded to keep her on, she really didn't belong in the inn—not where she'd be easy prey for any gentleman who had a bit much to drink. She should be working in private service. He snapped his fingers as a solution presented itself.

"Dry your tears, Poppy. As it happens my brother, the Earl of Granville, has a house in Chelmsford, very near Maldon, and I happen to know he is in need of a housemaid," Johnny said, blithely placing all of his dependence on his sister-in-law's soft heart. Juliana would find a place for the child.

She looked up at him dubiously, but there was a sparkle of hope in her blue eyes, still bright with tears. "Is Lord Granville truly your brother? A proper gentleman he is, my ma says. I seen him once and you don't look nothing like him."

"I should hope not," Johnny said, amused by her artlessness. "Spence is years older than I am. But he has recently married and has a little boy, and I imagine my sister-in-law could use some help with the infant. Do you know where Crowley is, then?"

She nodded. "My ma took me there once when she did some sewing for Lady Granville but that was afore she took sick," she said, remembering the spacious house and the beautiful countess who'd been so kind to her ma. Everyone liked Lady Granville—except for Prissy Allen—and that was only because she was jealous. Prissy had been the prettiest girl in the county until Lord Granville had brought home his lady. And now this young lord was actually offering her the chance to work there. It was almost too good to be true. She looked up at him, doubt in her eyes.

"Do you mean it, sir? Truly?"

"Absolutely. I cannot go with you—I've business to attend to—but if I give you enough for the stage and a letter to my brother, do you think you can find your way?"

For an answer, she enthusiastically threw her skinny arms about his shoulders.

At the same moment Miss Diana Talbot emerged from the steps and came round the corner of the hall.

Lord John, with his back to the stairs, did not see Miss Talbot approaching. And between Poppy's heartfelt expressions of gratitude and his own low chuckle, he did not hear her brisk footsteps or realise how damning his words sounded.

"There, poppet. You are a good girl and I shall see you have enough money to—" He broke off his words abruptly as Miss Talbot swept by him, her tiny nose tilted toward the ceiling and her skirts held tightly to her side. "Oh, Lord! Miss Talbot, I—"

She turned her head a fraction of an inch. Her eyes coldly noted his uncombed hair, his brocade dressing-gown and his bare feet. "You might at least have the decency to conduct your affairs in the privacy of your room, sir!"

"If you would let me explain," he began, but Poppy, suddenly realising how the scene must appear to the well-dressed lady, fell into a fit of giggles and clutched helplessly at Lord John's arm.

It was all Miss Talbot needed to see. Her breast heaving at such a blatant display of debauchery, she marched off, and a moment later the sound of her door shutting with unnecessary force reverberated through the hall.

"Oh, sir, it was so funny! Why, the lady must have thought that you and I—" She flushed suddenly and stepped away from him. The gentleman was not amused. "Is she a particular friend of yours, sir? Should I go and explain—"

"No," he interrupted hastily, visions of Poppy's garbled explanations making matters worse. "I shall straighten it all out with the lady later. You run along and get your belongings together and then come back here. By that time I shall have a letter ready for my brother."

She nodded and slipped off down the hall, nearly colliding with Jenkins coming up the steps with his master's breakfast. It was a struggle, but the valet managed to retain his grip on the tray and stared after the girl as she fairly flew down the steps. He muttered a few unkind words about the origin of her birth and tugged at his waistcoat with one hand. Dignity restored, he turned to find Lord John watching him and nearly dropped the tray again.

"My lord, you shouldn't be out here in the hall—not in your dressing-gown! What if someone was to see you?"

"Someone already has," Lord John replied, an odd smile on his lips. He strolled into his room and speaking over his shoulder, added, "Of course if you had been here instead of belowstairs gossiping, my reputation would not now be in tatters."

Jenkins protested, following him into the room and kicking the door shut with his heel. "I weren't never, my lord. I was just getting your coffee," he stopped, misliking the look of devilment in Lord John's eyes. "What's afoot? It ain't the Frenchie, is it?"

John shook his head and sipped the coffee his valet handed him. He chuckled softly. "No. I was thinking of Spence. You know my brother always said I never consider him when I'm abroad but I fancy I shall surprise him this trip. Find me some stationery, Jenkins. I must pen him a letter and, Lord, I'd give a monkey to see his face when he receives it!"

MISS TALBOT PACED her room. Her agitation was overpowering and she knew she could not face the others until she'd regained her customary composure. The sight of Lord John embracing that chambermaid in the hall—and in his dressing-gown no less—had affected her senses more strongly than she cared to admit. Of course, she told herself, it was merely her contempt for gentlemen who took advantage of helpless servants. Then honesty compelled her to admit the girl had not looked as though she objected to Lord John's treatment of her. Indeed, she seemed to be enjoying herself immensely. It was disgusting!

Diana took a deep breath, but the image of Lord John stayed with her. She could see his black curls falling over his brow and his sleepy, laughing eyes. The dressing-gown had left his chest partially bare, and she recalled all too vividly the way the dark hair had curled in tiny tendrils on his chest. For an instant, she had almost envied that ridiculous child clasped in his arms, very strong arms that could easily hold a woman captive. She shook her head. What in heaven's name was the matter with her?

She stepped to the window and allowed her gaze to focus on the sea. The rhythmic motion of the waves calmed her slightly. She knew what the problem was. The sight of Lord John had evoked all her memories of the Black Domino. She ached to be held in his arms again, to be soundly kissed until her senses were reeling....

"Diana? What are you doing, child? Mother is waiting below for us and you know how impatient she gets," Violet Talbot said, stepping into the room.

"I'm sorry, Mama," Diana said, turning from the window. "Has Lord Brownlow come down, then? Are we ready to leave?"

Violet nodded. "Though I shall be sorry to reach London. You know it will be more of the same when we get back. Mother is furious that you turned down Lord

Claypool and threatens to wash her hands of you. He's here now, did you know? I spoke with him just before coming up. Diana, he seems such a nice person...are you certain you cannot—''

Diana put an arm about her mother's shoulders and hugged her. "Not even for you, Mama, though I am sorry if it distresses you."

Her mother shrugged. "If you cannot bring yourself to accept his suit, then there is no more to be said, though I had hoped—well, it doesn't bear speaking of. And certainly not while Mother is waiting. And Lord Brownlow, too," she said, pausing to look up at her daughter. "He seems most eager to see you this morning, love."

"Does he?" Diana said, smiling. "Then let us not keep him waiting. I may yet surprise you, Mama."

"Diana! Do you mean—"

She placed a finger over her mother's lips. "Hush, dearest. It is far too soon to say anything yet, but I think you may hope—just the tiniest bit!"

They walked down the hall together, arms linked, and Diana spared only a brief glance at Lord John's room. The door was ajar and a chambermaid—not the little blonde she'd seen in his arms—was busily tidying the room.

Lady Throckmorton was waiting for them at the foot of the steps, leaning heavily on Lord Brownlow's arm. She nodded approvingly as Diana joined them. The girl's travelling dress was a pretty shade of lemon, embroidered with dark brown ribbons and lacing. Her hat, with its small, wide brim, was decorated with yellow and brown flowers, and had one long yellow plume that curled over her right ear. Diana carried a matching parasol along with a tiny yellow reticule that tied shut with brown ribbons. Delicate kid boots peeped out beneath her gown as she descended the stairs and extended a dainty, white-gloved hand to Lord Brownlow.

He bowed over her hand. "Ah, your fears about the weather may now be cast aside, Lady Throckmorton. We carry our own sunshine with us today."

Diana smiled. It was a pretty compliment. Unfortunately, her eyes strayed across the room to where Lord John was standing with Lord Claypool. Her eyes met his, and in spite of herself, she felt a hot blush colour her cheeks. She looked hurriedly away but not before she'd seen the amusement in his eyes. He was incorrigible, she thought, following her grandmother out into the yard.

Lord Brownlow's optimism aside, the day looked to be dismal. Dark clouds were already gathering and there was no trace of the sun. Lady Throckmorton was anxious to be off and they hurriedly settled in the carriage. Diana sat facing her mother and grandmother, with Lord Brownlow on her left. This was the gentleman she should be paying attention to! She enquired if he had slept well and when he replied pleasantly that he had indeed, though not for as long as he would have liked, she was unable to decide if there was any hidden meaning to his words.

She glanced out the window as the carriage rolled slowly forward and was amazed to see Lord John had come out into the yard and was standing there watching their departure. What cheek! He grinned as he caught her eye and then winked. The man was as bold as brass.

"Diana!" Her grandmother rapped her sharply across the knees with her cane. "Have your wits gone begging, girl? Lord Brownlow asked you a question."

IT WAS SOME HOURS before Lord John was able to follow them on the road north to London. He had seen young Poppy Beresford safely on the stagecoach, her thin

little hand tightly clutching the letter to his brother. It had
given him some small pleasure to induce Mr. Tibbs to
hand over the girl's wages. The overweight and unkempt
landlord had not done so willingly, but a few hints from
Lord John that the ton would not care to patronise an inn
that treated children so shabbily had been sufficient.
Tibbs had even offered to keep the girl on, but John had
smilingly declined what he termed the landlord's "most
kind offer." He knew full well the moment he left the
premises, Tibbs would throw the girl out.

The matter taken care of to his satisfaction, he had
strolled about the inn, paying particular attention to the
shrubbery, and had even paid a visit to the stables. There
was no sign of Lieutenant Jennot, though several of his
men seemed entrenched in the taproom. Perhaps the
good lieutenant had taken the hint, after all, and followed Brownlow. It was a pleasing thought, but John
remained on his guard. He believed it more likely that the
Frenchman was even now settled somewhere near Allington waiting for him. Well, Jennot would have his
work cut out for him. A proper storm was brewing.

It was close on to three when Johnny finally emerged
from The King's Arms, ready to travel. Finley had the
baggage strapped to the roof of the post-chaise and the
team of blacks were stamping their hooves and lifting
their heads in the nervous manner of high-strung horses.
A long drum roll of thunder sounded and flashes of
lightning lit up the sky. One of the horses shied, but Finley had it quickly under control. Lord John hesitated and
then nodded to his groom.

"Drive them as far as Maidstone and I'll take over. But
mind you, spring 'em. We've a deal of time to make up."

Lord John settled in the back of the luxurious carriage, intending to catch up on his sleep. Between the long

card game the night before and Poppy's waking him so early, he'd barely slept three hours. And he would need his wits about him if he was correct in guessing the lieutenant was hidden somewhere along the road waiting to ambush him. He could be wrong, of course, but he rather doubted it. It was the sort of thing he would have done in Jennot's place. Johnny closed his eyes and sighed, half hoping the lieutenant would have given up on him by this time.

They made good time through Ashford and Leeds, but then had to slow down as they approached Maidstone. The heavens had opened up and the rain came pelting down in torrents. The noise woke John and he sat up groggily. It was impossible to see anything out the window. He rapped on the roof with his cane and in a few moments the carriage rumbled to a halt.

John climbed out stiffly, oblivious to the rain. He never minded driving in a storm, for it had the advantage of keeping one alert. Finley and Jenkins were both drenched and John ordered them inside. His groom climbed down thankfully, tired from the long drive, but Jenkins remained on the box, turning a deaf ear to his orders.

Johnny eyed him and then grinned indulgently. It would take more effort than it was worth to shift his valet. Jenkins had been with him for too many years. He climbed up on the box and gathered the ribbons in his hands. "Where are we?"

"Just coming out of Maidstone, my lord."

Johnny nodded. Lightning flashed and he could make out the distant cliffs lining both sides of the road. Allington lay just ahead. He supposed he'd have to change teams there, though he hated driving with job horses. He'd hoped to make it to London with his blacks, but the storm was taking its toll and his pair looked pretty well spent. He couldn't risk it. If he had to make a run for it, he wanted fresh horses beneath his hands.

The road was dark ahead but at least it was paved. The new Macadam, and thank heaven for that. It made driving much easier but still he didn't push his team and was alert for any sudden movement. It was difficult to see with the rain coming in directly at them. Johnny shifted the reins to one hand and with the other pulled his beaver hat forward in an effort to shield his eyes.

He saw the dark form lunge across the road even as Jenkins shouted a warning and he swerved the team sharply to the right. The horses plunged wildly ahead, the carriage careening dangerously. It took all of his strength to haul on the reins. He cursed fluently, alternately checking and easing the ribbons until he brought the pair under control. He allowed them to trot for a quarter mile before he guided them to the side of the road and drew to a halt.

Lord John sat silently on the box, straining to see any movement beyond the falling rain. Jenkins started to speak but a warning hand laid tightly on his arm silenced him. John listened for several minutes but there was nothing. No sounds of pursuit or cries for help. He motioned for Jenkins to get down and whispered softly, "See to the horses."

He climbed down the other side and, with his pistol drawn, glanced round. He couldn't see beyond three feet but he didn't sense any presence and after a moment, he called to Finley.

Finley's head appeared in the window and the door opened a second later. The bow-legged groom jumped down, shaking his head. "And you've the nerve to complain about my driving!"

Johnny laughed, clapping him on the shoulder. "No need to ask if you are all right! Did I shake you up a bit?"

Jenkins came round the other side. "The horses are a bit spooked, but they'll do, leastways till we reach Allington. What the devil was that?"

"I am very nearly certain it was a horse," Johnny answered, staring down the road.

"A trap you think? Meant to drive us off the road?"

"Possibly, but then why wasn't it sprung? As far as I can see there's no one else about. No, I think something is very wrong. Climb in, Finley. I've a mind to investigate."

"Now, my lord, there's no call for you to do that," Jenkins protested. "You're already drenched through and we've still a few miles to Allington."

Johnny ignored him and turned to climb back up on the box. He looked down with a grin. "Are you coming, Jenkins, or shall I pick you up on the way back?"

Finley laughed and hauled himself inside the carriage while Jenkins mumbled unpleasantly, likening his master to a mule and other stubborn creatures. But in a matter of moments, he was seated beside Lord John on the box, though still grumbling.

"Like as not some farmer's horse has bolted and it has nothing to do with us, though telling you that will do no good. No, you'll have to go back and see for yourself. You're as bad as that girl and her dratted box of troubles."

John spared him a glance as he turned the horses, wondering if his groom was referring to Poppy, but she'd not had a box. Just a rather ragged valise with pitiful few belongings. "What girl?"

"That one Lady Granville was telling me about. Well, not me but that boy she has helping at the kennels, but I was a-listening. She said as how the girl wouldn't listen to no one and though she'd been warned not to do it, she opened the box anyway and all the troubles flew out."

"Oh, you mean Pandora!"

"That's the one, and only see what it got her. *She* wouldn't listen to no one, either. Had to go poking her nose in where it didn't belong and stir up a bunch of trouble when she could'a been sitting comfortable in a nice inn with a warm mug of grog."

Johnny smiled. "Never mind, Jenkins. As soon as we've seen if anyone's in need of help, we'll stop at Allington and you can have your grog. I give you my word."

They passed a bend in the road, and Johnny thought it was just beyond that the horses had bolted. He slowed the team to a walk, listening cautiously and wishing he could see better. The rain had eased a little, but night was drawing in and the road was pitch-black. He was about to give up when lightning lit up the sky. He saw the stallion in a grove of trees just off the road and reined in the horses.

"There!" Jenkins cried, pointing. "It was a horse, just like I said. Now, what are you doing?"

Lord John passed the ribbons to him. "We cannot just leave him there. Suppose he bolts again and causes a carriage to overturn? You stay here with the horses. If I can catch him, we'll tie him to the carriage and take him into Allington with us. Maybe we can find out who he belongs to."

"More like you'll be arrested for horse stealing," Jenkins warned, but without any real hope of being attended to.

The stallion, catching the scent of the blacks, nickered just as Johnny was about to cross the road. He paused by the carriage. He could swear there had been another sound. It had been faint, barely heard beneath the whipping wind and falling rain, but urgent. He stood still. It came again a moment later, a low moan. Johnny whirled about. It had come from a small stand of trees not a dozen feet distant from the carriage. He drew his pistol out and crept forward.

He'd not gone three feet when he heard Jenkins's whisper at his back. "Careful, my lord. It could still be a trap."

Thunder rumbled and Johnny waited for the lightning that would follow. The flash was brief but enough to see the man propped awkwardly against a boulder, his head hanging down so his chin nearly touched his chest. He motioned Jenkins to the left while he approached from the right, gun at the ready.

A second bolt of lightning blazed across the sky when Johnny was barely a foot away. He dropped at once to his knees, reaching out a hand to the injured man.

"Jennot! What's happened?"

There was no answer except a low groan.

"Get some brandy," Johnny ordered his valet. "And hurry!"

Jenkins was back in moments, uncapping a flask kept in the carriage. Johnny managed to get an arm round the lieutenant's shoulders and tilted the man's head back, pouring some of the brandy down his throat. Most of it dribbled down his chin but enough was swallowed so that Jennot sputtered and opened his eyes briefly.

"My leg," he murmured in French before closing his eyes. His head fell back against Johnny.

"I think he's been shot," Jenkins said, feeling along the lieutenant's leg. A makeshift bandage was tied tightly just above the right knee.

"Help me get him into the carriage," Johnny ordered, handing Jenkins the flask.

His valet knew better than to argue. He took a healthy swig of the brandy before recorking it and stuffing it in his coat pocket. Between them they half lifted, half dragged the Frenchman to the carriage. It was as well for Jennot that he was unconscious. He was no lightweight and it was a struggle to lift him into the post-chaise. Johnny propped him sideways on the cushioned seat, stretching his legs out in front of him.

"Leave me the brandy. I'll stay with him. You hold the horses and tell Finley to see if he can catch that stallion. But tell him not to waste any time—the lieutenant needs a doctor badly."

Jenkins nodded and disappeared. Johnny loosened the lieutenant's coat. Not his dress uniform but a large ill-fitting caped affair, the sort footpads wore. Small wonder he'd felt so heavy. The thing was sodden but there was no way to remove it now. Jennot looked dangerously ill and his head felt feverish to the touch. Johnny swore fluently.

There was a rap on the door and he pushed it open. Finley grinned up at him.

"Got 'im, my lord, and safely tied to the back of the carriage. What's to do?"

"Get us to Allington as quick as you can. There will be hell to pay if I have to explain how the lieutenant came to die in my carriage!"

CHAPTER FIVE

MRS. ALGERMISSON, proprietor of The Rose and Crown, had been all fawning servitude when Lord John strode in demanding the best room in the house. She had bowed as low as her wide girth enabled her to, and nodded her head so often that the faded blond hair twisted in a loose top-knot threatened to come undone. But her obsequious behaviour underwent a rapid change when she saw the wounded man carried in, trailing blood across her clean floors. It was obvious the fellow was half-dead and a death in the house was bad for business, and so she'd told the young lord. And bed linen was costly, she'd added, trailing him up the stairs. She could ill afford to have it bloodstained.

John had paid scant heed to her stream of protests as she'd followed them and ignored her when she trailed them into the room; but once he'd seen the lieutenant stretched out on the bed, he suddenly wheeled about, glaring at her so fiercely that she shut her mouth and retreated to the doorway.

"You will be well compensated for your trouble, madam, though your lack of compassion hardly does you credit," he said coldly.

"I saves my pity for them what deserves it," she retorted, nettled by the contempt and distaste she saw in his icy blue eyes. "And that don't include murderous highwaymen!"

Johnny, his gaze never wavering from her face, slowly removed his gloves. "And what, madam, leads you to believe this gentleman is a highwayman?"

"Plain enough to see if you have eyes in your head," she said, but under Johnny's unrelenting stare, hastily added, "My lord. Well, he's dressed like it and we was told one such was left shot in the road. Mr. Algermisson was going out to take a look as soon as the storm let up a bit. He promised the young lady."

"Indeed?" John took the few steps to the door, and drawing it shut behind him, backed Mrs. Algermisson into the hall. He towered over the landlady, but his eyes no longer looked so devilish mad and when he spoke, his voice was very nearly pleasant. "What lady was this?"

Mrs. Algermisson twisted the hem of her apron in her knobby hands. "I'm sure I don't know her name, my lord. She was just a young thing, travelling up to London with two older ladies. One might'a been a duchess or something—she had that air about her—and *she* didn't see no cause to be a-worrying over no highwayman, I can tell you. She told the young lady she was being foolish like, but the miss was insistent."

Johnny felt an unpleasant sensation in the pit of his stomach, but he gave no indication he was disturbed and guided the landlady down the steps. "I wonder, madam, did the young lady tell you what occurred?"

"Well, of course! She said as how they'd been set upon by a highwayman. He stopped their carriage just outside of town, but for certain he didn't count on the gentleman what was with them! He got no more than what he deserved if you was to ask me. They was ordered out of the carriage, but the gentleman shot the thief and the young miss said she saw the man fall from his horse."

"I see. And this gentleman just left the wounded man there?"

Mrs. Algermisson appeared indignant. "Weren't nothing else he could have done, my lord, now was there? He had the young miss with him and the older ones, too. Like as not, if he'd stepped out of the carriage, he would'a been set on by a whole passel of footpads. Besides, he stopped here to warn us."

"Ah, that was indeed kind of him," Johnny said, and knew she missed the irony in his voice. "Well, it appears there is some misunderstanding. I am acquainted with this gentleman and you may take my word for it that he is no highwayman."

She seemed about to protest, but Johnny produced a wad of folded notes and pressed them into her hand. "I want the best possible care for him. Send someone for a doctor at once. I will also require another room for myself, stabling for my horses and—" he paused, drawing out a gold fob and checking the time "—dinner in an hour or two."

Whatever she might think privately, Mrs. Algermisson was not about to offend a young lord as ready with his blunt as was this one. Her son was dispatched for the doctor and her daughter set about preparing a second bedchamber. She herself would tend to his lordship's dinner, she announced before waddling off to the back of the inn.

Johnny nodded and returned anxiously to the bedchamber, but there was little he could do. The lieutenant had not stirred since he'd lost consciousness in the carriage, and the pale form on the bed looked, as Mrs. Algermisson had noted, more than half-dead.

"I've got the bleeding stopped," Jenkins said. He bent over the bed, applying a cool cloth to the Frenchman's head, and then glanced up. "It would probably help if we could get him out of those clothes, but I wouldn't want to fuss him too much till a doctor sees him." He paused before adding gravely, "He needs a doctor mortal bad."

Johnny nodded, standing over the bed and staring down at Jennot. He had admired the Frenchman's resourcefulness and tenacity, and felt that under other circumstances, they might have been friends. But at the moment, the lieutenant was causing him a great deal of trouble. Johnny knew he should have been in London by now and the duke would be awaiting his report, but he could not leave Jennot like this. He cursed the Fates and wondered what was so bloody important about the papers he carried that Jennot had followed him to England and risked his life to retrieve them. He had gone well beyond the line of duty.

A rap on the door distracted him. A smaller, thinner version of Mrs. Algermisson entered and bobbed a nervous curtsy. "Dr. Wells is here, my lord," she said, and moved aside to allow a slender, dark-haired man to enter.

John greeted the sight of him with relief. He was younger than expected but he had a competent air about him and wasted little time on pleasantries. He nodded to John as he removed his coat, but his attention was already centred on the man on the bed. "Gunshot wound?"

"Yes, a...misunderstanding. The gentleman is French and here on the King's business. Whatever you can do for him will be greatly appreciated."

The doctor shot him a brief, sceptical look but vouchsafed no comment. He directed Jenkins to assist him and in a matter of moments tied a tourniquet above Jennot's knee and laid bare his calf, exposing a ragged wound. He sent the girl scurrying off to fetch a bowl of hot water and clean linen. Then, while rolling up his sleeves, suggested politely to Lord John that he might wish to wait below.

"I am not squeamish, Doctor."

"I was not implying you were, my lord, but I fancy I shall work better without your presence."

Johnny heeded what amounted to a polite order and waited impatiently in the taproom. It was near deserted, the inn being too close to London to attract many guests, and the local customers were kept away by the storm. He settled at a table after discovering the landlord kept a tolerable cellar, but neither the excellence of the wine nor the warmth of the fire was sufficient to still his fears. Mrs. Algermisson twice enquired if he was ready for dinner, but Johnny put her off. He wanted to hear what the doctor had to say before he dined.

It was close to two hours before Dr. Wells appeared, and the concerned look in his dark eyes did not bode well for the lieutenant.

Johnny motioned him to take the chair opposite and then asked, "Well, sir? How does our patient?"

The doctor shrugged. "He's resting, as comfortably as possible, but much will depend on him. Does he have a strong will?"

Johnny nearly grinned, thinking of the chase the lieutenant had given him, but answered somberly, "I think I may say that he does."

"He will need it. I've done what I could, but it's in the hands of God now. If he doesn't succumb to pneumonia, then he's a good chance, but lying in the rain for several hours..."

Johnny studied the strong face before him. Heavy lines were etched about the doctor's eyes and mouth and an overwhelming tiredness seemed to permeate his being. He was the sort who would take the loss of a patient hard. Johnny pushed the bottle of wine towards him. "Will you join me in a glass, Doctor? You look as though you've had a long day."

"Chickenpox," he replied tersely. "There's a small epidemic. I've been out for most of the day and had just sat down to dinner when the landlord's boy fetched me. You are fortunate he found me at home."

"Then the least I can do is buy you dinner, sir."

"It's not necessary, my lord. I wasn't hinting—"

"No, of course not, but I would consider it an honour. In return, you may tell me what I can do for my friend upstairs."

It was a poor bargain John struck. The doctor dined well but was unable to give him much advice. Keep the man warm, comfortable and when the pain was unendurable give him laudanum. He'd not held out a great deal of hope, advising Lord John that if he knew any prayers, he'd do well to say them.

Unable to sleep, Johnny had returned to Jennot's room. Jenkins quietly shook his head. There had been no change. John ordered him to get some rest and settled himself in the large wing-chair near the bed. He dozed off once or twice, coming wide awake when the lieutenant moaned or stirred restlessly.

It was near three in the morning when Jennot finally opened his eyes. He lay still, watching Johnny asleep in the chair, and then enquired softly, "My lord?"

Johnny was awake instantly and on his feet. He hurried to the side of the bed. "So! You are conscious at last. How are you feeling, Lieutenant?"

"Thirsty," he said, his throat feeling raw.

Johnny poured a glass of water and supporting the Frenchman beneath the shoulders, lifted him so he could drink.

"*Merci*. Where . . . where am I?"

"At The Rose and Crown, just as you come into Allington. I found you lying beside the road with a bullet in your leg."

Jennot groaned, and Johnny eased him down on the pillow, intending to give him a dose of laudanum, but the lieutenant reached for his hand.

"It was . . . Brownlow. I do not understand why he fired. . . ." he murmured in French, looking up at Johnny with feverish eyes.

"Is it not rather obvious? If he is the Domino—"

"No!" The denial burst from the lieutenant's lips. He closed his eyes at the pain it cost him and tightened his hand on John's. "The Black Domino would not have left me there to die like an animal."

The words were so softly spoken that Johnny had to lean close to the lieutenant to hear them, and even then he was not entirely certain he'd understood the rapidly spoken French, but any doubts he had were quelled when Jennot opened his eyes again. Compelling dark eyes that stared fiercely into John's own.

"This changes nothing, my lord. I owe you my life, but my first loyalty is to my sovereign. You would have done better perhaps . . . to have left me in the road."

"Very possibly," Johnny said, straightening up. "Especially if you persist with this mad delusion of yours. For now, however, I must oblige you to take your medicine. Someone most wise, one of our generals I believe, once said that the man who knows when to retreat may live to fight another day."

Something very like a smile twisted Jennot's lips. "French," he murmured. "A Frenchman said it first."

THE MORNING FOUND the lieutenant more improved than Johnny would have believed possible. The man had a will of iron and was more stubborn and determined than anyone John had ever met. The Frenchman had even tried to get out of bed. It was the noise of his fall that had roused Johnny. He smiled over his breakfast, recalling the scene.

He'd helped the lieutenant back into bed and then demanded to know why he'd tried to get up. "If there's anything you want, you've only to ask, Lieutenant."

Jennot fought to regain his breath. The exertion the effort had caused him had left him near exhausted. Still, he half smiled and when he could speak again, glanced up at John. "I doubt you would have been so obliging as to hand me your pistol, my lord."

Johnny's brows shot up. "And then what, my dear Lieutenant? Would you have been so crass as to shoot me?"

"A little, perhaps," he'd murmured.

Johnny had laughed. "Your gratitude is overwhelming, Lieutenant. We English would consider it rather beyond the pale to shoot a man while wearing his nightshirt."

"I would regret it immensely, but more is at stake than I think you realise.... Have you read the papers you carry?"

Johnny's eyes danced with amusement. "I see I shall have to summon the good doctor again. You are still suffering delusions."

"It is you who are deluded. If those papers reach the wrong hands it could mean another war between our countries. Then, many more lives would be lost. In such circumstances, neither you nor I hardly matter."

"Speak for yourself, Lieutenant. I value my life dearly."

"Oh, of course," he'd answered dryly. "No doubt that is why you risk it so frequently. You are... reckless, my lord, but I think—a man of conscience?"

"I know a number of people who would most certainly dispute with you on that head—in particular, my brother," Johnny said, hoping to keep the conversation light. It was becoming increasingly difficult to deny the Frenchman's accusations. "He deplores my activities, you know, and quite cringes when someone refers to me as Madcap Johnny in his hearing."

Jennot would not be diverted. "There are those in power who are not satisfied with the results of the Vienna Congress...men who speak of forging new alliances and some who have been so foolish as to put their thoughts in writing. Rulers who are dissatisfied with the way Poland and Saxony were cut up... They look to France for assistance, but my country is tired of war. We want no part of such alliances."

"I fail to see the problem, then."

"The papers would make it appear France is in league with these men against England."

Johnny whistled. "No wonder you are so determined! A pity it is out of your hands now, but I think you underestimate the English, Lieutenant. Our leaders are not given to leaping to conclusions, and England wishes for war no more than France."

It was the Frenchman's turn to raise a pair of sceptical eyebrows. "The Prince Regent?"

Johnny grinned. "Granted he has not a brilliant head, but he is well advised by very knowledgeable gentlemen.

Now, shall I send for your men? I must be off to London today, though I am loath to leave such charming company."

Jennot nodded. "I shall return to France. There is nothing more I can do here, but I wish . . ."

"Yes?"

"I wish you would burn those papers."

Johnny laughed again and moved round the bed towards the door. "Is there nothing I can say to convince you that I am not the man you seek? I do wish I might oblige you, but—" He broke off, shrugging. "I really must leave. There is a young lady in London most eager for my company. That, I know, you will comprehend."

Johnny had left him, retreating to the taproom for breakfast, but quite certain he had not convinced the lieutenant of his innocence. Jennot was a formidable opponent, he thought, sighing over his coffee. It was just as well that this was his last trip as the Black Domino.

DIANA ALLOWED Lord Brownlow to hand her down from the carriage. She was relieved to be home and looked up at the grand house in Manchester Square with relief. The drive from Dover had been a taxing one in spite of the viscount's entertaining company. He'd done his best to amuse the three ladies and was succeeding very well until the incident at Allington. Diana shivered as she remembered the vision of the highwayman falling from his horse.

Brownlow noticed and was at once all solicitous concern. "Are you chilled, Miss Talbot? I pray you are not coming down with a cold."

"Nonsense," Lady Throckmorton announced, descending behind her. "Diana is too sensible to catch a fever. I daresay she is merely tired from the drive, though I feel perfectly well and rested.''

"It is the dampness," Violet said, placing a comforting arm about her daughter's waist. "I feel it myself. What we need is a nice fire and a hot cup of tea to take the chill off."

"Tea we shall certainly have, though I don't hold with coddling. You'd do better to take a brisk walk about the square and get your blood moving, Violet."

The door was opened by the elderly butler before her daughter could reply and the ladies ushered in with due ceremony. Brownlow declined an abrupt invitation from Lady Throckmorton to remain for tea, pleading pressing engagements. But when he turned to take his leave of Diana, he bowed over her hand, holding it longer than might be considered proper.

"It has been a pleasure, Miss Talbot. I hope you will allow me to call tomorrow and see for myself that you've incurred no illness."

"Thank you, my lord," she replied, conscious of her grandmother watching them. "I should be pleased to see you."

Lady Throckmorton nodded, well satisfied, and then directed her retainer to see tea was served at once in the salon. "Diana, I wish to have a word with you as soon as you've put off your travelling dress."

"Yes, Grandmama," she said, and turned up the wide stairs, thankful that she would have at least a few moments alone before facing the inquisition she knew awaited her. She wished she knew what she might say to her grandmother, but she was at a loss to explain her own feelings.

Annie, the maid she shared with her mother, was waiting and helped her to change into a simple white muslin day dress. Its only adornment was a narrow blue ribbon laced through the high waistline and repeated across the sleeves, but its simplicity suited her. Diana cleansed her face carefully and allowed Annie to run a comb through her curls. It didn't do to appear before her grandmother less than presentable. She stepped into the hall and encountered her mother.

"You look lovely, darling, though a little pale. Are you certain you are feeling perfectly well?"

"I am fine, Mama, just a trifle tired. Are you coming down to tea?"

Violet twisted the handkerchief in her hands nervously. "No, Mother wishes to speak to you alone. Dearest, try not to—"

"Don't worry, Mama," Diana interrupted, taking both her mother's hands in her own. "Whatever her threats, Grandmama will not turn us out into the street." She leaned forward and kissed her mother on the cheek. "Try to rest a little, and I shall come up later. We will have a comfortable talk, just the two of us."

Her mother nodded, but the worried look was still in her eyes when Diana left her. She hurried down the stairs, wishing there were something more she could do for her mother. It was unfortunate that they'd little choice but to live with Grandmama. For herself, she didn't mind, but with each year that passed her mother seemed to grow more frail, more nervous until the light-hearted, cheerful young woman Diana remembered from her childhood had all but disappeared. If only Mama would stand up to her, she thought. Grandmama admired strength of character and Diana had tried to tell her mother so. But Violet Talbot was a timid creature and above all things she hated any sort of quarrel and was reduced to tears if anyone so much as raised his voice to her—something which Grandmama did frequently of late.

Simmonds, her grandmother's personal maid, emerged from the salon just as Diana was about to enter. In her own way, Simmonds was as bad as Lady Throckmorton. She disapproved of both Diana and her mother and had openly resented them coming to live in the Square.

"There you are, miss," she said now, her thin lips pursed in tight disapproval. "Her ladyship sent me to find what's keeping you."

"Thank you, Simmonds," Diana said, smiling cheerfully at the elderly woman, knowing it was the most effective way of dealing with her. The maid sniffed but dared make no further remark and Diana stepped into the salon.

Lady Throckmorton might declare she did not hold with coddling oneself, but no one would have guessed it at that moment. The fire burned brightly, providing a welcome warmth and a lavish tea was laid out near the sofa where her grandmother was seated comfortably, a rug over her lap and her three fat and rather spoiled pugs sprawled about her.

The one nearest Diana raised his wrinkled head and growled as she bent and dropped a kiss on her grandmother's brow.

Little beast, Diana thought, seating herself in the adjacent chair and waiting patiently while her grandmother caressed and soothed the pug.

"You may pour the tea, Diana," Lady Throckmorton said without looking up. Her attention was all on the dogs. "I fear my girls are a little out of sorts, Drucilla in particular. Simmonds told me they would hardly touch a bite of food while I was gone."

"I shouldn't think it would hurt them," Diana said, passing a cup to her grandmother. "It may even do them some good. You know they are entirely too fat."

"Which shows you know nothing of the matter, miss. Pugs are naturally plump and these three are excellent specimens. Furthermore, they are far more worthy of your concern than some nameless highwayman!"

Diana busied herself with filling a plate, carefully keeping her eyes averted. She had anticipated a lecture on what her grandmother had termed her unseemly conduct.

"Well? Have you nothing to say?"

Diana raised her eyes and smiled. "Nothing you would wish to hear, Grandmama."

"Your behaviour was abominable, Diana. All that fuss and commotion over a common thief, and insisting we stop to send someone to help the fellow. I cannot imagine what Lord Brownlow thought."

"Very likely that I am a tender-hearted girl who cannot bear to see a man shot and left to die in the road like a dog."

"Hush, Dulcie," Lady Throckmorton said as the pug to her left issued a low growl. "A dog would have been more deserving of your compassion. The man was a common thief."

"Whatever his calling, he is still a human and does not deserve to die like that."

"Hmmph. Would you rather see him hang?"

"Of course not, and neither would you," Diana answered with an impudent grin. "What concerns you is that I offended Lord Brownlow, but he has forgiven me. Did you not hear him ask to call on the morrow?"

"He may well call tomorrow, but you'll lose him in the end if you don't mend your ways, my girl. It's bad enough to have lost Claypool—though I don't blame you there for a more namby-pamby foolish coxcomb I never saw—but the Brownlow is a different tale. Let him slip through your fingers and I shall wash my hands of you."

As you have done a dozen times in the past, Diana thought, watching one of the pugs licking her grandmother's fingers. Secure and pampered, the dog turned his head to look smugly up at her at the same instant as her mistress and Diana was struck by the resemblance of the two wrinkled faces. She couldn't help smiling.

"You think it amusing, do you? Well, you won't think so when you find yourself governess to a brood of noisy brats, which is the fate awaiting you now, my girl. You've had more chances than most and whistled them down the wind. Too proud by half. The least you could have done was to thank Brownlow for defending us. Heavens, any other girl would have been in raptures. It's the stuff those penny romances of yours are made of!"

Not quite, Diana thought, remembering how rapidly Brownlow had produced the pistol. He had waited until the highwayman had turned to the side and then fired without warning. The man had never had a chance. And when their coachman had made to climb down, Brownlow had ordered him to drive on and seemed surprised when she'd protested.

"Hand me one of those macaroons," Lady Throckmorton directed. "You would have thought differently had that man succeeded in holding us up. Brownlow was quite right to put our safety first."

"Of course, Grandmama, and I did apologise, only..."

"Only what? Give over, Diana, and admit you botched the affair. You acted as though he'd done something criminal, when you should have been praising his lordship and swooning over his bravery. That is the sort of behaviour that brings a gentleman up to scratch.''

"But I do think he is brave," Diana protested. The Black Domino was the bravest gentleman she had ever heard of. She struggled to explain her ambivalent feelings and spread her hands helplessly. "I suppose it is just that seeing a man actually shot is so wretchedly different from reading about it.''

Lady Throckmorton swept the crumbs from her chest and looked at her granddaughter. Diana's troubled eyes mirrored her confusion and the old lady's features softened. Perhaps after all there was some justification for the child's behaviour. She smiled at the girl. "Well, I daresay you may be forgiven for being a little faint-hearted. Just make certain that tomorrow you properly praise his lordship.''

"I shall try, Grandmama.''

"Turn him up sweet, Diana. You marry Brownlow and I will leave everything to you. You have my word on it.''

"And if he does not offer?" Diana couldn't resist asking, though she knew it was foolish of her to tease her grandmother.

Lady Throckmorton frowned, but a discreet rap on the door forced her to hold her tongue. "What is it?" she demanded.

One of the footmen stepped in and, with an apologetic air, announced Mrs. Bottomham wished to see her ladyship.

"Show her in," Lady Throckmorton ordered and glanced triumphantly at her granddaughter. "There's your answer, Diana. Obey me, or everything shall go to your cousin.''

Emily Bottomham minced in, her pudgy figure swathed in yards of crimson satin that did nothing to flatter her figure. Diana watched as she greeted her great-aunt, all breathless and gushing effusively, and was reminded of an over-ripe tomato. Emily, two years younger than Diana, had succeeded in marrying Horace Bottomham six months earlier. He was not a magnificent catch, but that didn't prevent her from flaunting her married status over Diana every chance she got.

The cousins exchanged a light airy kiss and polite greetings but Diana saw Emily's furtive glance at her hands. The relief in the girl's eyes at seeing no ring was patent and her high, squeaky voice took on an added note of glee.

"Oh, you have the darling doggies with you. I daresay they missed you terribly. Pugs are such devoted creatures, are they not?" she said to her great-aunt and tentatively stretched a hand towards the one in Lady Throckmorton's lap.

The pug took exception and bared his teeth in a menacing growl, much to Diana's approval. Emily snatched her hand back and hastily took a seat near the fire.

"Well, I just had to come and hear all about your trip. I was saying to Mr. Bottomham this morning that we must go abroad ourselves one of these days, and of course he instantly promised to take me. I declare I never knew being married could be so pleasant. The dear man positively spoils me. I have only to utter a wish and the thing is done. Really, Diana, it is such a pity you never married, for I do assure you it is a most delightful state."

"I can see it agrees with you, Emily," Diana said, handing the girl a cup. "Have you put on weight, my dear? They do say that is a sign of contentment."

Emily giggled and blushed, not in the least offended. "How very perceptive of you, cousin, to guess my secret. That is the other bit of news I came round to tell you!" She turned to her great-aunt and modestly lowered her large hazel eyes. "Mr. Bottomham and I wanted you to be the first to know, Aunt Henrietta." She looked about as though to be certain no one else was listening and then whispered, "I am breeding."

Diana nearly choked on a sip of tea, but Lady Throckmorton looked over the rim of her cup and nodded approval.

"Well done, Emily. I am most pleased."

"And dear Mr. Bottomham said I might tell you that should it be a girl, she will be christened Henrietta, and if it is a boy, then we shall call him Henry in your honour."

Diana sat quietly, listening to her grandmother's delight at the coming child and asking questions about the attending physician. She was full of recommendations and advice, and more than once Emily looked at her cousin with sly triumph.

Diana rose at last, unable to bear any more. "I know you will excuse me, Emily, if I leave you alone with Grandmama. I am sure you have much to discuss, and I am rather tired from our journey."

"Oh, quite, Diana. There are things I want to ask Aunt Henrietta that you, as an unmarried woman, really should not hear and besides, you look a bit wan."

"I know," Diana sighed. "And I do want to look my best tomorrow when Lord Brownlow calls." She had the satisfaction of seeing her cousin's mouth fall open.

"Brownlow? I did not realise you were acquainted with his lordship."

"Yes," Diana said with a sweet smile. "We met him in Dover, and he was obliging enough to give us his escort back to Town. Really, his attention was most flattering and he insisted on calling tomorrow." She waited, knowing Emily would find something unflattering to say about him. She always managed to imply that any gentleman calling on Diana was less than respectable.

"I should be careful, if I were you," Emily said, and turned to her aunt. "Mr. Bottomham has told me things—rumours, which of course that I cannot repeat in front of Diana—but Brownlow is . . . well, reckless. A dangerous man for someone like my cousin to know."

"You should not pay heed to idle gossip, Emily. Lord Brownlow comes from an excellent family. I knew his grandparents personally," Lady Throckmorton said, frowning down her nose at her niece. "I find him perfectly acceptable."

"And so do I," Diana said, smiling at her grandmother before sweeping from the room.

CHAPTER SIX

IT WAS PAST three o'clock when Johnny, looking tired, dusty and disheveled, arrived at the Duke of Cardiff's Town residence in Belgrave Square. He was admitted by Thurgood, the duke's imposing butler, and shown to a sitting-room. Not by so much as by a flicker of an eyelash did the butler betray any dissapproval. There was no frown—in fact no trace of any emotion at all on Thurgood's wooden countenance—but he felt the butler's censure all the same.

One glance about the elegant room and Johnny decided to remain on his feet. He wondered if Thurgood had shown him there deliberately. There had been several occasions in the past when he'd had to cool his heels while waiting to see the duke. Those times, he'd been shown into a small but comfortable salon near the duke's library.

"His Grace will see you now," the butler intoned from the doorway. "If you will please follow me, my lord."

Johnny was startled. He'd not heard the butler approach, but he covered his surprise and appeared at ease when he turned, murmuring politely, "Thank you, Thurgood."

The butler led the way down the long hall, lined with windows on one side, and surprisingly cool and quiet in the late afternoon. Johnny followed in his wake, speculating on whether the competent Thurgood did more for the duke than merely running his household. The man moved with extreme quiet for a person of his size, Johnny thought, listening to the clatter of his own boots against the marble floor.

Thurgood tapped discreetly on the door of the library before opening it and announcing Lord John.

The Duke of Cardiff stood waiting behind the massive oak desk and Johnny forgot all thoughts of Thurgood. The duke might not have his butler's impressive height, but he had a commanding presence that demanded total and complete attention.

"Well, John?" he asked, and indicated with a wave of his arm that his visitor should be seated. He took his own seat, leaning his grey head against the high back and allowing his aristocratic hands to rest on the curved arms of the chair. "I am pleased to see you are not injured. I was concerned when we had no word of you yesterday. Was there trouble?"

"In a manner of speaking, Your Grace," Johnny said, uncomfortably aware of the dark, intelligent eyes inspecting every inch of his body. "A French lieutenant followed me to Dover."

The duke's heavy, shaggy eyebrows rose a fraction of an inch above his hooded eyes. "The papers?"

"Safe, though they near cost the lieutenant his life," Johnny replied after only the barest hesitation. He withdrew the packet from his coat and tossed it on the desk.

Cardiff made no move to touch it but kept his gaze fastened on Johnny. "He would be neither the first nor the last to lose his life in service to his country. It is a risk we all take, and if you were compelled to use force against him—"

"Oh, I was not the one to put a bullet in him," Johnny interrupted and proceeded to quickly outline what happened, carefully omitting his encounter with Miss Talbot and ending his tale with Jennot's plea that the papers be destroyed.

His Grace was not pleased. Johnny knew it though the duke had not uttered a word. The silence in the room became a palpable thing, and he had to resist a strong urge to blurt out some foolish justification for his actions.

"This rather complicates matters," the duke said at last. He rose stiffly and walked to the windows flanking his desk, and stood staring out at the sweeping view of the gardens. "I could wish you had not chosen to involve yourself with the lieutenant's rescue, though I understand your motives."

"I could hardly have left him to die in the road," Johnny said, coming to his feet.

"No...of course not," Cardiff murmured. He turned and a sudden smile softened his features and warmed his eyes. "We cannot have French corpses littering our roads. Someone would be bound to object."

Johnny smiled, as he was meant to, but it was a poor effort and the duke noticed.

"What bothers you most, John? The fact that the lieutenant seems certain of your identity or that he risked his life to prevent those papers from reaching me?"

Johnny looked away from the sympathetic grey eyes and shrugged lightly. "As this was my last trip to France, it can scarcely matter what the lieutenant suspects."

"We shall discuss that shortly," the duke said, returning to his seat. He looked at his guest for a long moment and then reached up a hand to tiredly rub the back of his neck. "We have known each other for a long time, John, so let us not fence. What are you keeping from me?"

Johnny felt a surge of affection for the older man and regretted what he had to say, but honesty compelled him to meet the duke's eyes and speak frankly. "I want to re-tire, Your Grace."

"I see." There was neither surprise nor censure in his voice. He turned in his chair, reaching behind him for a brandy decanter and two glasses. He poured them both a measure and pushed a glass across the desk before he spoke again. "Was it the lieutenant's eloquence that in-duced this change of heart, or something more?"

"I suppose Jennot may have had something to do with it, but not entirely. I have felt for some time that I should like to resume a more normal life. You are aware my brother has been urging me to settle down and marry, and I admit the notion is not unappealing."

"That is understandable," the duke said, nodding. "But you could still do that—play a less active role."

Johnny shook his head. "I think not. I could see some point to spying on France while we were at war, but now...I am sorry, Your Grace, but I am not altogether convinced that we are acting wisely and, feeling that way, I consider it is best I withdraw. I have given seven years of my life in service to Crown. Surely that is enough?"

The duke shrugged. "Who can say? I've given thirty years and there is still much to be accomplished. Our mission did not end with the war, John. The Crown still has need of loyal men."

"Then perhaps it is my loyalty that is in question," Johnny said softly, staring into the untouched glass of brandy. "I do not know whether you can understand this, but I no longer feel certain that what I do is...justified."

Cardiff took a sip of the brandy and then sighed. "I suppose there is no more to be said, then."

Johnny looked down at his hands. He had expected this interview to be difficult, but the disappointment in the duke's voice filled him with remorse and he almost regretted his words.

"I should like to ask one last favour," the duke said quietly.

"Anything in my power, Your Grace," Johnny offered eagerly, looking up at the man who had so influenced his life.

"Do not be so quick to agree," the duke said with a half smile. "It will take a little time to replace you, John. Your rather unique talents have been invaluable to us. Indeed, I can think of no one else at present who is as capable—but there remains a job that must be done."

Oh, damn, Johnny swore silently. He should have known.

"One last trip abroad and then, I promise you, you may retire with my blessings."

"To France?" he asked with dismal foreboding.

The duke nodded gravely. "There is a gentleman in Versailles who has been most instrumental in providing us with accurate information. Unfortunately, we've received word that he has fallen under suspicion and is now being held prisoner. We must get him safely out of France."

"Versailles! You are not asking much," Johnny said, shaking his head at the enormity of it.

"You see why you are needed, John. There is no one else I'd trust with this. I would not ask it even of you, but this gentleman knows a great deal about our organisation. If we leave him to the French . . . well, the lives of many men could be in danger."

"When would I have to leave?" he asked, resigned.

"In a fortnight, I should think. I am making arrangements now."

Johnny took a sip of the brandy, mourning the loss of his plans and wondering if something yet might be recovered. He looked across at the duke, speculation in his blue eyes. "Might I be granted a favour in return, Your Grace?"

"What is it?" Cardiff asked with a guarded look.

"I have met a young lady.... She is very high-minded and I fear my cover as a madcap has been most effective. She views me as a rather frivolous, contemptible fellow, but I should like to tell her the truth. She can be trusted," he added hurriedly as he saw the duke frown. "Her father lost his life on the Peninsula and a young man she was nearly engaged to died at Vittoria."

"I am sorry, John, but you know it is impossible. Even the duchess does not know the extent of my activities. It's too risky," he said with a frown. "This lady could betray us without ever meaning to. A slip of her tongue, an unguarded look—no, I cannot allow it."

Johnny nodded. He had hoped the duke might make an exception, but had not really expected it. But how in the devil was he to convince Miss Talbot of his worthiness in a fortnight?

He spent two fruitless days trying to think of a solution to his problem and even confided in his friend George Somerset, but to no avail. All George could suggest was that he call on Miss Talbot. Johnny morosely pointed out that even if he found her at home and were granted an interview, there was nothing he could possibly say to the lady that would change her opinion of him.

THE LADY who so troubled his thoughts went blithely about her business, unaware of his concern and only occasionally thinking of him. On Wednesday, she called on an old school friend and was greeted warmly. They settled in the sitting-room, and after refusing all offers of tea and cakes, Diana leaned back in her chair, smiling. "I want nothing but to be allowed to sit here and listen to you tell me all about your wedding trip—but I warn you, one word that you are with child and I shall be out the door!"

Venetia Courtland laughed, transforming a fairly attractive face into a delightful one. A row of small white teeth showed beneath delicately curved pink lips and two dimples suddenly appeared. Her green eyes took on an added sparkle, making her look absurdly young, though she was the same age as Diana. The pair had been close friends since attending school together and Venetia was used to Diana's outrageous remarks.

She lifted a hand to push a tendril of coppery hair away from her cheek and said, "I promise you there is no reason for you to desert me just yet, but surely it cannot be as bad as you would have me believe. Emily always seemed such a quiet mouse of a girl."

Diana nodded with mock gravity. "We were grossly deceived."

"Perhaps her enthusiasm will wane," Venetia suggested. "No doubt it is the newness of the experience and she cannot help speaking about it endlessly. I expect I shall be equally loathsome when my time comes."

"Never will I believe that. Oh, Venetia, you must think me horridly mean-spirited, but truly I don't begrudge Emily her bit of happiness. It's just the way Grandmama and even my own mother fuss over her. It is all they talk about. To hear Grandmama speak, one would think Emily has performed some amazing feat. It's as though she were the first woman to ever get herself with child!"

Venetia leaned forward and patted Diana's hand. "In Emily's case, perhaps it *is* amazing. I own I was quite surprised to hear she had wed. What is he like?"

"Oh, you should ask Emily. She is an authority on Horace Bottomham and cites him on every subject. It is Mr. Bottomham said this and Mr. Bottomham thinks that and on and on until I think I shall scream."

"Well, if you won't take tea, perhaps you would like a dish of cream," Venetia suggested, her eyes full of mischief.

Diana was taken aback for an instant but then smiled ruefully. "I quite deserved that. I am turning into a malicious cat, and can barely speak civilly to my own cousin. And if matters are at such a point now, only think what it will be like once the dear child is born. I shall likely have to be committed to an asylum."

"I think there may be an easier solution," Venetia said, passing a cup of tea to her friend. "Drink that. It will help settle your nerves. Have you considered marriage yourself? That would certainly put your cousin's nose out of joint."

"That is the crux of the matter. Grandmama is miffed that I turned down Lord Claypool and even Mother thinks he is a dear, sweet man—which I freely admit he is. I know he would have done everything in his power to make me happy, but—I could not do it. Venetia, you understand, don't you? If I must marry, I should at least like my husband to be someone I can admire."

"Of course I do, darling. I never thought Claypool the right man for you. Your grandmother must be losing some of her wits if she thought a match could be made there, but is there no one else?"

Diana was silent, tracing the rim of her delicate cup with the tip of her finger. "There is someone I have met—"

"Tell me instantly," Venetia cried, setting her own cup down and leaning forward eagerly.

Diana shrugged. "There is hardly anything to tell as yet, but I did meet a gentleman in Dover and he escorted us back to Town. Apparently he was abroad for some years which is why I have never met him before, but Grandmama knows his family and is pleased to encourage him. Indeed, she has said that if I marry him, she will leave me her fortune."

"Your grandmother should choke on her gold," Venetia said. "I have told you before, Diana, you are welcome to come live here whenever you choose and you may tell Lady Throckmorton what she can do with her money."

"I know and I am grateful but Grandmama means well and . . . this time I might wish to oblige her."

"What?" Venetia said, her brows arching in surprise. "Who is this paragon? Why, Diana, you are actually blushing."

"Hush. I do not wish to exaggerate what may be a mere courtesy, but he has called twice and yesterday he took me driving in the Park. I think he is someone I could . . . admire very much. His name is Simon Yorke," she said, her tongue lingering over the name. "Viscount Brownlow. Are you acquainted with him?"

Venetia busied herself with the teapot and did not look at her friend as she answered. "I believe I met him some years ago."

"Out with it, my dear," Diana said, watching her closely. "I can see you are biting your tongue."

"It is nothing…just some rumours I chanced to hear,"
Venetia said with a graceful wave of her hands. When
Diana continued to sit silently staring at her, she added,
"Did he tell you why he spent so much time abroad?"

Diana knew a measure of relief. She had braced herself to hear something terribly damaging about the viscount. But this was nothing. She knew why he had stayed
in France, though it was hardly the sort of thing you
could tell a friend over a cup of tea. Not even a friend as
dear as this one. She smiled at the concern in Venetia's
eyes. "If that is all that is troubling you, I think you need
not be worried."

A deep masculine voice called a hello from the doorway, and Venetia was saved from answering. Thomas
Courtland strolled in, looking unusually mature in for-
mal morning attire. He was still the same boyish Tom,
however, and pulled Diana to her feet and hugged her
warmly without the slightest concern for his elegantly tied
cravat. She had been the one to introduce him to Venetia
and he claimed to be forever in her debt.

He released her with a laugh. "I'm delighted to see you
here, my dear. There's someone I've been wanting you to
meet." He turned to his wife with a wide grin. "You will
never guess who I met this afternoon!"

They heard the door open again and Tom strode towards the hall. "Come on, Johnny, what's keeping
you?"

Lord John Drayton stepped into the hall. "You must
allow a man to see to his horses, Tom. I can understand
your impatience to see your bride again, but—" He
broke off his words as he entered the sitting-room and
saw Diana.

She unaccountably blushed and looked down at her
hands.

"Diana," Tom said, placing an arm about her shoulders. "I should like you to meet one of my dearest friends, John Drayton. Johnny, this—"

"I have had the honour," Johnny interrupted. He saw her glance up and bowed slightly. "It is an unexpected pleasure to see you again, Miss Talbot."

"Thank you, Lord John," she murmured, and could not explain the nervousness that tied her tongue like a shy schoolgirl's.

She had a chance to compose herself while he said hello to Venetia, and was able to reply almost rationally when he asked politely after her mother and grandmother. His words were unexceptional. The sort of casual talk any gentleman might have made, but something about Lord John left her feeling unsettled. Perhaps it was his penetrating blue eyes. A sudden vision of him as she'd seen him at the inn, his dressing-gown open nearly to the waist and his hair tousled from sleep, disordered her thoughts and she turned in some confusion to Venetia.

"You will stay for dinner, will you not?" her friend was asking. "Both of you? It will give Tom and me great pleasure."

"I cannot, though I should love to," Diana said, drawing on her gloves, and trying unsuccessfully to ignore Lord John. "We are promised to Lady Hereford tonight, and if I do not return home at once, Mother will be sending round to Bow Street to hunt me down."

Diana collected her maid and Tom offered to see them safely out, but it was Johnny who usurped his place and walked out with her to the carriage. She was uncomfortably aware of him beside her, and thankful for Annie walking a step or two behind.

"I hope it is not my presence here that sends you hurrying off, Miss Talbot," he said, as they halted before the brougham.

Diana raised her brows. It was very nearly the truth, but such conceit! "Really, my lord, I fear you over estimate your importance. Your presence—or absence—can hardly be thought to dictate my actions." The carriage door was open and he held out a hand to assist her up the steps. Reluctantly, she placed her gloved hand in his.

"One can always hope, Miss Talbot," he replied softly.

JOHNNY DECLINED the invitation to dinner as well and returned to his own apartments to find a note from Spencer waiting for him. His brother desired him to call in Cavendish Square when it was convenient. Jenkins informed him the note had been delivered early that morning by the earl's footman and, anticipating his master's wishes, had laid out fresh evening dress for his young lord.

His brother's presence in Town was something Johnny could have gladly dispensed with, but he knew he would have to see him, and there was little point in procrastinating. He had a deep fondness for his elder brother, but Spence was certain to scold him over that business with the ballerina.

He considered what he might say in his defence while he changed his dress, replying in monosyllables to Jenkins. The charade the Duke of Cardiff had stage-managed to provide Johnny with an excuse for leaving England at once had been all too effective. Lord Wincanton, another of the duke's minions, had enacted a memorable scene at the Royal Opera House. In front of a dozen or more gentlemen, he had loudly and offensively insulted Johnny for his treatment of Peggy Rad-

cliff, the little ballerina who was the current sensation.
Johnny had naturally called him out, and with gentlemen carefully selected by the duke to serve as seconds, the
mock duel had been fought the following morning.

Rumours had quickly spread, undoubtedly aided by
the duke's efficient staff, that Lord Wincanton had been
fatally wounded, and Johnny had just as quickly taken
himself off to France. After Johnny was safely abroad,
Wincanton had let it be known that his wound was a mere
scratch and was heard to lament his haste in calling Lord
John out. It was all a mere misunderstanding, he said,
and no hard feelings. He was even heard to express his
admiration for Lord John's prowess with the sword.
Everyone had a good laugh over it and no harm was
done, save for George's hurt feelings at not being asked
to serve as second. George, of course, had forgiven him,
and had taken great delight in roasting him unmercifully
for his frantic flight abroad.

Spencer Drayton, the fourth Earl of Granville, was not
likely to take such a light view of the affair. He was a se-
rious-minded gentleman who found little to amuse him
in his brother's escapades and much to exasperate him.
Although marriage to pretty Juliana Chevron had considerably altered his habitually somber conduct, nothing
could change the utter contempt in which he held duel-
ling and he was certain to lecture his younger brother se-
verely.

There were times when Johnny frequently wished that
his brother would not concern himself so readily in his
affairs, but he knew Spence to be devoted to him. Spence
had been only fourteen when their parents had died, but
he had taken on the role of father and mother to eight-
year-old Johnny, with a seriousness and dedication rare

in so young a boy. And little had changed in the intervening years.

Johnny sighed, tying his cravat with a carelessness that appalled Jenkins, and wished, not for the first time, that he could confide in Spence the truth about his activities. The duke, however, had strongly forbidden it. Cardiff knew how much the earl secretly admired his younger brother's unquestionable courage, and feared Granville would not be able to hide his pride if he knew Johnny's exploits were a mere cover for his real activities on behalf of the Crown.

He had said on more than one occasion that Granville's disapproving lectures lent a credence to Johnny's cover that was invaluable. Johnny acknowledged it to be true, but that was scant consolation when he had to face Spence and see the disappointment in his brother's eyes.

He was still trying to think of an adequate explanation to placate Spencer when Hadley admitted him to the earl's residence an hour later. He knew a moment's relief when the butler informed him that his lordship and the countess were sitting with Lady Guilford.

"Aunt Georgia here? Wonderful!" Johnny had no need to feign his pleasure at the news. He knew he could count on his aunt's support, and her reputation as a madcap was nearly as infamous as his own. She had never seen anything amiss with his activities, and more often than not delighted in hearing of his escapades. The time he'd held up Lord Cochrane's coach, his diminutive aunt had clapped her hands with unabashed glee and demanded a first-hand account, much to Spence's annoyance.

Hadley formally announced him at the door of the sitting-room, but Johnny brushed past him and scooped his two-year-old nephew up from the floor, lifting him playfully above his head.

"Uncle Johnny," the boy gurgled happily, wrapping his chubby pink arms about his uncle's neck and landing a sloppy kiss on his cheek.

"Johnny," Juliana cried with real delight and rose to meet her brother-in-law. "Do put him down before he ruins your coat."

He ignored her advice and kept the little nipper in his arms while he kissed her cheek. He then turned to his aunt, his eyes dancing with amusement, and offered his hand. "Aunt Georgia, this is an unexpected pleasure. When did you return? How is Guilford?"

"We returned last week, and Charles is divinely happy, of course."

"Of course," he acknowledged with a wicked grin. And it was probably true. Although Georgia had neatly manoeuvered Charles into proposing and had completely disrupted his well-ordered existence, his new uncle still seemed to consider himself fortunate in winning the former Lady Alynwick.

He felt a hand on his shoulder and turned to find Spence beside him.

"I am glad to see you safely back in England, John—"

"Spencer," Georgia interrupted, languidly waving her fan, "if you are going to prose on in that odious censuring voice just like your uncle used to do, then I shall take my leave at once."

Little John Louis let out a wail the same instant and his lower lip trembled ominously as he stared at his papa, his blue eyes filling with tears.

"Let me take him," Juliana said, lifting her arms to the child and directing a reproachful look at her husband, but the child buried his face in Johnny's cravat and tightened his arms about his neck.

The earl shook his head. "It is a conspiracy. I cannot even welcome my brother home without—"

"It was the tone of voice you used," Georgia interrupted from her place on the sofa. "Obviously, the prelude to one of your scolds, but really, darling, you would do better to wait till you are alone with Johnny, unless of course you wish to spoil my visit and upset your son?"

Johnny grinned and carried his nephew to a chair near the fire, murmuring nonsense in his ear until a gurgle of laughter erupted. "You have another uncle eager to see you, little one," Johnny said, and looked across to Juliana. "Your cousin is the most amiable of fellows, and sends his love to you. He can hardly wait to see you again, and his namesake, of course."

"I knew you would like each other," she answered, smiling. "I only wish I could have gone with you. It has been so many years since I've seen Louis. I hope he is well?"

Spencer returned to his own chair while they were chatting and, under the guise of sipping his tea, watched his son with amusement. Already the boy had destroyed his brother's stylish hair and was rapidly making a mess of Johnny's elegantly tied stock. He set it to his brother's credit that he was unconcerned with his appearance and the thought came unbidden to mind that if his son turned out half as well as his brother, even with all his faults, he would be well pleased.

Juliana, returning to her seat near her husband, reached out and briefly touched his fingers with her own, smiling affectionately at him. Her attention was diverted when Johnny suddenly groaned. She turned her head and realising the situation, stifled a laugh.

"You little devil," Johnny said, lifting his nephew down to the floor and using a handkerchief to mop hastily at the wet stain spreading on his buff pantaloons. "Have you no manners? Let me tell you, my boy, in polite circles such conduct is considered quite inappropriate."

John Louis, his attention distracted by the tassels on his uncle's boots, reached out a chubby hand.

Juliana rose and pulled the bell rope to summon her son's nurserymaid and then hurried across the room. "I did warn you, Johnny," she said to her brother-in-law while taking the little boy's hand. "You are much too indulgent with him."

"Now don't go taking him away on my account. The damage is already done," he replied, looking down at his ruined stock and pantaloons. His black Hessian boots, so glossy when he had entered, now bore tracks of little fingerprints.

A maid entered hesitantly. "You rang, my lady?"

Johnny glanced up at the old woman. Her face was lined with heavy wrinkles, and wisps of thin grey hair hung listlessly from beneath her mob cap. Her shoulders hunched forward as though she bore the weight of the world on her slender frame.

"Sarah, could you please take John Louis up and change his clothes," Juliana asked, leading the little boy across the room.

The child's face screwed up and turned red as he uttered a loud wail of protest.

"Here, now," Johnny objected.

"He will be fine," Juliana said firmly, closing the door after Sarah and blocking out John Louis's lusty cries.

"I say, Juliana, isn't she a bit old to have charge of the boy? The woman looks exhausted."

"No doubt because she is," his sister-in-law answered, resuming her seat. "It is the most vexing thing, but the nurserymaid we had suddenly gave notice and I have been at wits' end to find a suitable replacement. Sarah offered to help, but I fear it is too much for her."

"If the child is anything like Johnny and Spence when they were boys, you will need a much younger woman," Georgia murmured. "I remember once when Spencer was left alone, he got into his mother's oil paints and completely redecorated the nursery. And his brother," she added with a reminiscent smile.

"Yes, well, it is most difficult," the earl said, to change the subject. "We have advertised but no one in the least suitable has applied."

Johnny, standing near the fire in the hope his pantaloons would quickly dry, accepted the cup of tea Juliana brought him. "I think I may have just the person for you," he said, remembering the chambermaid he'd sent down to Crowley.

Georgia raised her blond brows. "You are acquainted with a nurserymaid? How very extraordinary."

"He keeps rather strange company, as you should know, Aunt," Spencer said dryly.

She was instantly defensive on Johnny's behalf. "If you are talking about that ballerina, let me tell you that there is a vast difference between a gentleman knowing such a person and knowing a nurserymaid. Really, Spencer—"

"If you will allow me to explain," Johnny broke in. "I chanced across a young girl at a place I was staying in Dover. She'd been given notice by the landlord because she wouldn't..." He hesitated, uncertain how to proceed in front of his aunt and Juliana. "She, er, kicked a gentleman who refused to accept that she'd no desire to visit his rooms."

"Oh, the poor child," Juliana cried, remembering all too vividly an unpleasant encounter with a lascivious employer.

"Nevertheless, however sorry we might feel for this girl, I hardly think she would be appropriate," Spencer said, and at Juliana's frown, added, "and it would be impossible to find her now."

"Not at all," Johnny said, grinning. "She's at Crowley."

"What?"

"Now, Spence, only listen. She's just a child, a poor skinny little thing, but she's helped to rear four younger ones and she comes from Maldon." He appealed to Juliana. "She says her ma did some sewing for you before she took sick. Name's Beresford. Anyway, the girl was stranded and I sent her on to Crowley, thinking you could likely use some help."

"Yes, of course," Juliana murmured. "She must be Lucy Beresford's girl." She turned to her husband, her green eyes shining with compassion. "Do you not remember I mentioned I must call on her one day? I had heard she was terribly ill and meant to do something, but with John Louis..." She turned back to Johnny. "You did very right to send her to me, and I will write Mrs. Jamison at once and have her brought here."

"How domestic you are becoming, Johnny," his aunt remarked idly as she examined her ivory fan. "Finding nurserymaids and playing with your nephew. It's very affecting to see you with a child in your arms." Her eyes peeped innocently up at him beneath long lashes, and with soft waves of blond hair framing her delicate oval face, she resembled an angel.

"Up to your matchmaking again, Aunt Georgia?" he asked, undeceived, but smiling at her efforts. "Do you never admit defeat?"

"Never," she owned. "And I chance to be acquainted with a young lady who would be most suitable for you."

Johnny hesitated, wondering if perhaps his aunt could be of some assistance, and after a few seconds, he said with an air of unconcern, "Well, if you've a mind to meddle, there is one young lady I would be pleased to have you ask for dinner."

For all his casual air, his comment astonished his family and Juliana and Georgia both spoke at once, demanding to know the paragon's name.

"Miss Talbot," he said slowly, already regretting his impulse. He turned to his brother, missing the look of absolute horror on his aunt's face. "She's Lady Throckmorton's granddaughter, and they've just returned to Town."

"Oh, no, darling," his aunt replied in considerable agitation. She rose and crossed to his side, laying a compelling hand on his arm. "Pray tell me you are only jesting. Miss Talbot will never do!"

CHAPTER SEVEN

"WHAT POSSIBLE OBJECTION can you have to Miss Talbot?" Johnny asked, masking his concern behind a lazy drawl. "I was not aware you were even acquainted with the lady."

"I am not on terms with her, if that is what you mean," Georgia said, acutely embarrassed at the position she found herself in. She stepped away from her nephew, plied her fan to cool her flushed cheeks and took a seat beside Juliana. "Perhaps I should not have spoken, but it would be a dreadful misalliance if you were to marry into that family."

Spencer sat quietly back in his chair observing the scene. His aunt had schemed for years to marry Johnny off, with a notable lack of success. He glanced at his wife, remembering that Aunt Georgia had once intended Johnny to wed Juliana. Or so she'd said. He still occasionally wondered if the elaborate hoax they'd enacted had really been for Johnny's benefit, or if Aunt Georgia had meant Juliana for himself all along. She had been strangely unsurprised when Spencer announced their engagement. With Aunt Georgia one never knew. He watched her jewelled hands moving expressively as she talked. Was this another of her endless matchmaking schemes, or did she really have some objection to Miss Talbot?

"The family are all eccentrics," she was saying. "Violet Pennington, the girl's mother, married against her family's wishes—some soldier or other without a shilling to his name who was killed on the Peninsula—and then she had to return home. Lady Throckmorton took her in, of course, but not willingly and has since made her life a misery if only half the tales one hears are true."

"But that hardly makes her daughter ineligible," Juliana said softly, reaching for her aunt's hand. "My own family was as bad."

"But it did not affect you, darling," Georgia said, squeezing her fingers. "Though Miss Talbot is dependent on her grandmother, she seems to disoblige her at every turn. She has had plenty of offers, but the only one she ever considered was a soldier, another just like her father, and he was killed in one of Wellington's campaigns before they could wed—which is perhaps just as well. I do not mean to sound heartless, but Lady Throckmorton was dead set against the match and it would have never done. Since then Miss Talbot has received half a dozen good offers and rejected every one."

"Perhaps she is merely discriminating," Johnny suggested.

"Stubborn," Georgia corrected, her pretty lips set in a firm line. "She could have married any time these past few years and been settled comfortably, but she seems to delight in thwarting her grandmother. Eccentrics, the pair of them. It is like a game they play. After each refusal, Lady Throckmorton drags her back to Bath and threatens to disown her. She will do it, too, one of these days, mark my words. She'll leave everything to that dreadful niece of hers—a horrid pudgy child with no manners at all. The only thing one may say to *her* credit is that she managed to get herself properly married."

"How perfectly dreadful," Johnny said, leaning against the mantel and watching his aunt with considerable amusement. "But I know you too well to believe that lack of a fortune would weigh with you. Out with it, Aunt Georgia! What is your real objection to Miss Talbot?"

"Laugh if you will, but I am warning you, Johnny, she would make us all terribly uncomfortable. I do not blame the girl, of course, not with her upbringing, but she has turned into the most..." She paused, searching for a word, her expressive hands fluttering helplessly. "She disapproves of the most harmless pleasures...."

Even Spencer was beginning to be amused, and sat hiding his smile behind his teacup.

"Where did you meet Miss Talbot, Aunt Georgia?" Johnny asked, determined to find out what was behind his aunt's curious behaviour.

"At the Devonshires'," she replied, distracted.

Juliana heard the earl murmur softly, "The child travels in the first circles. The Duchess of Devonshire, no less..."

Georgia, who in her agitation was nervously pleating the skirt of her pale blue silk, looked up to find three pairs of eyes closely watching her. "Oh, she has the requisite breeding! 'Tis just her manner. The duchess arranged a harmless treasure hunt, but Miss Talbot would take no part in it. Nor would she consent to dance in the drawing-room or to sit down for a rubber of whist, or play the spinet...there was no pleasing her and she cast an incredible pall over the entire party. I can remember Her Grace was at a loss how to entertain her. She scorned the other young ladies who were present and conversed only with one or two military gentlemen who were quartered in the area."

"Perhaps she was merely uncomfortable with her position as Lady Throckmorton's pensioner," Juliana suggested, remembering her own retiring behaviour at several of her grandfather's parties.

"If that were all," Georgia said, her pretty cheeks flushing, "I could forgive her. But the way she looked at me when she encountered me in the garden with the Duke of Clarence—" she broke off abruptly, realising her tongue had betrayed her.

"Flirting with the duke, were you?" Johnny said with a laugh. "And probably still married to Uncle at the time, I'll wager!"

"It was all perfectly harmless," Georgia declared, "And nothing would have been remarked if Miss Talbot had conducted herself with a little more propriety. To go running back into the house, her face flushed with embarrassment..." Her own face flooded with colour as she recollected the scene. "That little miss rushed through the drawing-room, refusing to speak with anyone, and of course when Clarence and I stepped through the door a moment later, every eye in the room was staring in our direction! Your uncle was utterly mortified, and had I been with any gentleman other than a Royal Prince, I believe he would have demanded satisfaction."

"A pity he didn't," Johnny said irreverently. "We might have been rid of the old windbag sooner."

"Yes, darling, but only think of the scandal! As it was, your uncle sent me to stay with his sister in Bath for the rest of the Season and nothing could have been more uncomfortable."

"But surely this was all some years ago," Juliana pointed out reasonably. "And no doubt Miss Talbot was a shy and very sheltered young lady at the time. Do not tell me you still hold her to blame?"

"Not I," Georgia said, looking affronted that she should be thought so uncharitable. "You know my forgiving nature! No, it is Miss Talbot who frowns down her nose at me and makes clear her disapproval every time we chance to meet. I encountered her at Lady Castlereigh's ball last year and the look she gave me—well!" She turned to Johnny with an imploring look. "I simply could not bear it if you married her, darling, and I know in my heart you would come to regret it immensely. If you have a mind to settle down at last, I know a perfectly charming girl...."

Spencer judged it time to interrupt. He stretched out his long legs, dislodging the spaniel sleeping on top of his boot. "I rather think this girl precisely the sort Johnny needs. It is perhaps too much to hope that she might have a sobering influence on him, but if she can curtail some of his more outrageous exploits, I should be well pleased," he said, casting a quelling look at his aunt as she moaned.

"It is what I fear," she murmured to Juliana.

"Shall we invite Miss Talbot to dine?" Spencer asked, ignoring his aunt as he rose and crossed to Johnny's side.

"If you can manage it, I should be pleased, but I fear all this talk of marriage is a bit premature," his brother answered with a lopsided grin. "The thing is, she don't like me above half."

WHILE JOHNNY DID NOT overestimate Miss Talbot's opinion of him, he would have been deeply hurt had he heard her, several days later, confiding to her friend Venetia Courtland that she thought him an amusing rogue, but with no substance to him.

"Just as I told Tom," Venetia replied with no little satisfaction as their carriage halted in front of a mercer's shop on Ludgate Hill.

A gentleman usher, richly and colourfully dressed, waited to hand them down and directed their attention to the gilded door. "Have you need of Garden silks, ladies? Italian silks; we have very fine mantua silks, today."

Diana smiled sweetly at him and they entered the shop to find his two partners waiting to flourish out the silks. It was not in her mind to make a purchase, but she couldn't resist fingering some of the exquisite material.

Seeing her interest, one of the gentleman stepped forward. "This, madam, is wonderfully charming, a most diverting silk." He gathered a length to form a sleeve and held it up against her shoulder. "My stars! How becoming it looks against milady's face. It suits you wondrously well."

Diana reluctantly shook her head. Fifteen shillings a yard was much too dear for her purse.

"Offer him ten," Venetia advised.

"How unkind of your ladyship to rally me," he retorted. "Ye gods, the weavers would revolt were I to part with it for less than fourteen."

"Even at ten shillings I could ill afford it," Diana owned, and reluctantly stepped away. She waited patiently while Venetia made her purchases and then strolled with her friend towards Number 32, the goldsmiths and diamond merchants, Rundle & Bridge. The day was cool, but the sun was shining and the ladies walked leisurely.

"Whatever made Tom think of Lord John?" Diana asked curiously. "Is he a particular friend?"

Venetia nodded absently, waving a gloved hand at Mrs. Drummond as her carriage rumbled by. "I believe they have been acquainted for years, and belong to the same clubs. I confess I find him devilishly handsome, and as you say, quite amusing, but not, of course, the sort of gentleman that one would take seriously. A pity, but he is a confirmed bachelor and it must be beyond the hope of any lady to bring him up to the mark."

Diana raised her delicate brows. She privately thought it might not be beyond *her* ability, were she so inclined, but of course a lady must not utter such thoughts, and she contented herself with remarking that he'd been most attentive when they were in France.

"I suppose it is well that you are so sensible, Di, and did not allow yourself to be charmed by his good looks. I can think of no one less suited to you."

"No, indeed," Diana agreed as they were bowed into Rundle's. She knew Venetia meant the words kindly, but she was a trifle miffed and had the feeling her friend thought her incapable of bringing Lord John to heel, should she choose. It was foolish, of course, when she had no real interest in the gentleman, but the feeling persisted.

Venetia enquired for Mr. Rundle, but had to be content with the services of Mr. Quimby, a mere clerk, the proprietor being occupied in his office with a gentleman. She reluctantly produced her emerald necklace, but made it clear to the clerk that it was Mr. Rundle himself who had sold the piece to her husband, and she had been much dismayed to find a stone loose in the setting.

He was quite as appalled as she could have wished, obsequious in his attention and promised to have the necklace repaired promptly and without charge. He flattered her, calling her "my lady" several times and asked if she had seen the exquisite diamonds just received.

Venetia, well pleased, condescended to look and was at once entranced by the gems. She begged Diana to come admire a particularly fine diamond brooch. The ladies were extravagant in their praise and Mr. Quimby suggested they move near the door so "madam might see how exceptionally the stone glistened in the sunlight."

His effusions were cut short. Loud cries of alarm were heard from the street and what sounded like thousands of thundering hooves drowned out his protests when Diana stepped towards the door. She stared in utter amazement.

Drivers were whipping their horses into a panic trying to clear the street as dozens of cattle pursued them, and gentlemen and ladies on foot were running into every open door seeking shelter. Even as Diana watched, one gentleman's tilbury overturned and he was thrown to the ground, while his plunging horses dragged the equipage on down the street.

Wild shrieks of fright were heard from the ladies, and not a few gentlemen, and the hysterical barking of dogs as they ran alongside the cattle, furiously braying and nipping at their heels, added to the confusion. The herd of cattle covered the width of the cobblestoned street and two roughly clad young men with stout sticks ran along the pavement on either side, cursing them soundly, and doing their best to keep the maddened animals from turning into the buildings.

Diana stared in fascination, hardly realising the peril she was in. Her attention was focussed on a scruffy young boy, his head bleeding profusely from a cut, who was running directly towards her. She could clearly see he was in danger of being run down by a bull and could think of no way to prevent it. Impulsively, she stepped out onto the pavement and reached out a hand to him. She had just grasped his coat when she felt a masculine arm reach round her waist and haul her back into the store.

Thrown abruptly off balance, but without losing her hold on the boy, Diana fell heavily against the gentleman. The three of them tumbled backwards onto the floor of Rundle & Bridge in a tangle of arms and legs. Mr. Quimby stood above them, his eyes bulging with astonishment, too shocked to utter a word.

It was Venetia who hurriedly stepped forward and tried to assist Diana to rise. Her cheeks were suffused with colour, for Diana's ankles and a goodly portion of her legs were displayed in a most unseemly manner. Her efforts were useless, for the gentleman, whom she recognised instantly, had his boot firmly planted on the skirt of Diana's lilac walking dress and the grubby urchin was sitting practically between her legs.

"Oh, do get up, Diana. Your *limbs* are showing!"

"I am fortunate they are not broke," she replied and urged the boy to try to stand. She turned her head to beg her rescuer remove his boot as well as the strong arm still encircling her waist, but the words died on her lips as she looked into the saucy blue eyes of Lord John.

He grinned unabashedly and rose gracefully to his feet. His eyes did not miss the pretty display of leg and were full of mischief as he extended a hand to help her up. "Miss Talbot, your servant. How utterly delightful to see you again, and how fortunate I had business here with Rundle."

One had to admire his composure, she thought, and accepted his assistance in rising.

He bowed to Venetia as though nothing untoward had occurred and enquired pleasantly after Tom.

"He is well, my lord, and—good heavens, Diana, there is blood on your skirt! Are you injured, my dear?"

"I do not believe so. I rather expect it is from this waif," Diana replied, and reached out a hand to stop the boy edging towards the door. "Have you no manners? You should at least say thank you, young man. Had it not been for my intervention and that of Lord John, you surely would have been trampled."

He flushed to the roots of his red hair, and hung his head. A jagged cut marred his forehead but he seemed more nearly concerned with his stomach. His coat there bulged beneath his arms and to Diana's astonishment, moved alarmingly.

"He should be handed over to the watch," Mr. Quimby blustered, assuming a position of authority once more now that danger to the shop was passed. "No doubt he was throwing stones at the cattle or something and stirred them up. That's why they were chasing him!"

"Is that true, lad?" Johnny asked, his voice holding a note of sympathy that brought the boy's head up.

"No, sir," he mumbled, his large brown eyes as round as saucers and full of fear. "I wouldn't do nothin' to hurt the cattle."

Venetia quietly took Diana's arm and whispered, "If you are certain you are not harmed, let us return to our carriage."

"In just a moment," Diana said, and knelt before the boy. "What have you in your coat?"

The lad moved his hands slightly and the head of a black-and-white mongrel puppy, as scruffy as the boy himself, peeped out. "It's jest my dog, miss."

"I see," she said softly and reached a hand to caress the pup's head. It cowered beneath her touch. She could see the poor thing's body was so thin the ribs showed, and it was quivering with fear. "He seems fairly frightened."

"Yes, miss. He crawled under the fence and the cattle was going to stomp him. I got 'im jest in time but..." He broke off, ducking his head.

Lord John stepped behind her and looked down at the boy. "I'll wager the cattle saw you and stampeded. Was that it?"

The boy nodded miserably and Quimby again inserted his opinion the waif should be turned over to the watch. "There are severe penalties for stampeding cattle and no doubt a great deal of damage has been done."

"He's just a child," Diana said sharply, rising to her feet and looking contemptuously at the clerk. "Do you seriously expect him to pay damages?"

"It would be a lesson to him and the others," he insisted, puffing out his chest. "That's what the law is for."

Lord John drew out his card case and proffered several of his calling cards. "The law would do well to order Smithfield Market moved beyond Town limits. It is entirely too close and little wonder the cattle frequently stampede—with or without this lad's help. However, should you hear of any damages, you may direct enquiries to me."

"My lord, there is no reason why you should—" He broke off under the haughty gaze of Lord John. "Well, if that is what you wish, of course, my lord."

"It is exceedingly kind of you," Diana said, turning to Johnny, her eyes aglow with an unexpected warmth. "But what do you intend to do with the boy?"

"Do with him? Why, nothing. Send him home, I suppose," Johnny said and glanced at the boy, only to find a pair of large brown eyes gazing hopefully up at him.

"I doubt he *has* a home," Diana observed quietly, having taken note of the boy's painful thinness and shabby dress. "However, if you could find some employment for him—tending your horses, perhaps, or in the kitchen—"

"Miss Talbot, if mine were not a bachelor's household, I should be glad to oblige you, but you must see—"

"Yes, I do see, and pray spare me your excuses! You are like all the other fashionable gentlemen who deplore all the orphans on the street but do not lift a finger to assist them. Never mind. I shall try to prevail upon my grandmother to take him in. Come along, Venetia."

"Diana! Are you mad?" her friend whispered furiously, glancing apologetically back at Lord John. "You know Lady Throckmorton would never agree to such a scheme."

"I shall think of something," she replied, lifting her chin. "I am acquainted with at least one gentleman who I believe might be prevailed upon to help a small homeless boy."

Lord Brownlow, Johnny thought and cursed silently. If he had a grain of sense, he'd let her take the boy to the viscount and then see how saintly that gentleman proved to be. The problem was, knowing Brownlow, he would likely sell the lad off first chance he got.

He coughed and stepped forward, laying a hand on the boy's shoulder. "I beg your pardon, Miss Talbot, but you did not allow me to finish. I was about to say that while I maintain only bachelor quarters, my brother, Lord Granville, is now in Town and I am quite certain he can find some sort of employment for the lad—that is, if he is indeed an orphan."

The waif grinned up at him, bobbing his head. "It's just me and Rags, sir. My pa ain't been round since it snowed last."

"Well, where are you living, then?"

The boy shrugged, and ducked his head. "Here and there," he mumbled.

"There are hundreds like him, my lord," Diana said softly. "They take shelter where they can and scrounge food from dustbins. It is all so distressing, and no one to speak on their behalf," she added and paused, eyeing Lord John speculatively. "If you could but persuade your brother to address the matter in the House of Lords..."

His lips quivered. He could just imagine the look on Spencer's face were he to propose such a thing. He managed not to laugh outright and concluded that Miss Talbot's passion could be used to his own advantage. "Obviously, you are well informed on the subject. If you would but consent to dine with us one evening, I am certain my brother would be moved by your eloquence."

The lad stirred beneath his hand and scratched listlessly at his head while watching the adults converse above him. Johnny prayed he did not have fleas or lice or some such thing.

"I—I should be pleased, of course," Diana murmured, realising how adroitly she had been manoeuvred, but it was for a good cause. She extended her hand graciously. "Thank you, Lord John, and I believe I have been remiss in not expressing my gratitude for your rescuing me. It was well done of you."

"My pleasure, Miss Talbot," he said, executing a neat bow while maintaining a firm hold on the boy. "Mrs. Courtland, your servant."

She nodded pleasantly and the ladies stepped towards the door.

"Oh, Miss Talbot? If you are agreeable, perhaps I might call tomorrow and tell you how our orphan here has fared?"

"If you like, sir," Diana agreed, rapidly thinking. Lord Brownlow had been asked to tea, but she would wager her grandmother would not be displeased if Lord John were to join them also. "Come at four o'clock," she suggested with a warm smile and then yielded to the insistent pressure Venetia was placing on her arm. "I bid you good day, sir."

As soon as they were out of earshot, Venetia scolded her. "What are you about, Diana? Did we not just agree an hour past that Lord John was entirely unsuitable? I own myself astonished that a lady of your intelligence would allow herself to be blinded by a handsome face, though you are not the first—"

"Oh, do hush Venetia! I am *not* as you put it, blinded by his good looks." Her words were not as forceful as she would have desired, and she owned silently that Lord John was uncommonly handsome.

"Indeed?" Venetia replied, unconvinced. "I saw the way you smiled at him, my dear! And if you have some notion that the gentleman is not as black as he has been painted, and offered to take in that child out of the goodness of his heart, you are much mistaken!"

"Of course I do not. His reputation as a madcap is no doubt much deserved. We chanced to stay at the same house while I was in France and I had ample opportunity to observe him, and a more worthless, idle gentleman I have never met. No, I am aware he acted merely to oblige me, but what matters is the opportunity to lay the problem before his brother. Lord Granville is respected in the House, and if he were to address the matter of the orphans, something might be done. Lord John may think to use the poor child to impress me, but I mean to use his lordship for my own purpose."

Venetia shook her head. "I fear you are making a vast mistake, Diana, and Lord Brownlow may not take kindly to your encouraging Lord John to dangle after you."

"Perhaps that, too, can be turned to good account," she answered, a tiny smile turning up the corners of her mouth.

JOHNNY WASTED NO TIME in calling on his sister-in-law. Hadley, for all his vast experience, was unable to keep his double chins from quivering with astonishment when Lord John was admitted to the hall, trailed by the veriest urchin.

"Afternoon, Hadley," Johnny greeted him, handing over his cape and hat to a waiting footman. He motioned to the boy half hiding behind him. "This is Alfie. Be a good fellow and take him to the kitchens. He needs a good meal and—" he paused, glancing at the boy again before adding in a low voice "—and if you can manage it, a bath would not be amiss."

"My lord," the butler protested, staring aghast at the child. "I cannot—"

"I don't expect you to see to it personally, Hadley, but surely my brother has enough servants in this place that he can spare one to tend to this lad. Is my sister-in-law at home?"

"Yes, my lord. She is in the salon, but—"

"Wonderful, Hadley. I'll announce myself. You may bring the boy there when you are done." He strolled down the hall before the butler could protest further and knocked lightly on the door of the salon before poking his head in.

"Johnny! Do come in," Juliana said, rising and crossing the room to bestow a light kiss on his cheek. "Spencer is at the House of Lords, though I expect him back soon, and little John Louis is sleeping. I find myself utterly bored and wishing we were back at Crowley where there is always so much to be done."

He followed her back to the sofa and took a seat while Juliana rang for refreshments. It was several minutes before they were both comfortably settled and he took a sip of sherry. "Not enough for you to do in London, is there?"

"No," she sighed. "And with Spencer so busy...well, I do not mean to complain."

"I may have a solution to your problem," he said. "A small project for you to take in hand."

Juliana, acquainted with her brother-in-law for several years, knew well the look of mischief in his eyes. "What are you about, Johnny? If it is anything that will disturb Spencer, I warn you—"

"Now, why must everyone always think I do ought but stir up trouble?"

"Experience, perhaps?" she asked, smiling at his wounded air.

He grinned. "Well, this time I cannot be faulted. Indeed, I think you will approve. The thing is, I found this urchin on the street. A quiet, well-mannered boy, but he's an orphan. No place to stay and scrounging round for food. He is painfully thin, Juliana, to the point where his bones show through his shirt. And he has no clothes, save what's on his back, and that half in tatters."

"The poor child! How came he to be orphaned?"

"To say the truth, I haven't asked. You see, he stampeded the cattle at Smithfield—an accident of course—"

"A quiet, well-mannered boy, did you say?"

"I did, and I am certain you will agree—once he is cleaned up," he added conscientiously. He told her in detail what had occurred and that were it not for Miss Talbot, the poor little boy would have been seriously injured.

"I believe I am beginning to understand," Juliana said, smiling at the mention of Miss Talbot as she refilled his glass.

A loud crash sounded in the hall and they both looked up expectantly.

"What the devil—" the earl's voice roared ominously and somewhere a dog was barking furiously.

Johnny stirred uneasily in his seat and looked at Juliana. "Did I mention Alfie has a dog?" he asked as he stood.

"Oh, good heavens," she cried and followed him to the door.

The Earl of Granville was sprawled unceremoniously on the floor of the hall, amidst pools of water and dozens of flowers from an overturned vase. Felix, his favourite spaniel, barked hysterically, chasing a mongrel pup round his lordship's body, and sliding on the wet floor. The pup, his tail between his legs and his body quivering with fear, dashed beneath Spencer's knees.

Hadley, along with several footmen, stared in horror.

Spencer grabbed the pup by the scruff of its neck, ordered Felix to cease his attack and attempted to rise. He was instantly knocked down again as a young boy, clad only in water and a few stray soapsuds, raced down the hall and collided with him.

Juliana leaned weakly against the door. She could not help laughing and she looked at Johnny with tears of mirth in her eyes. "A quiet boy, you said?"

CHAPTER EIGHT

LADY THROCKMORTON, enthroned on the sofa with two pugs on her lap and numerous shawls draped round her to guard against drafts, was feeling particularly pleased. She watched the two young gentlemen, confronting each other like a pair of wary alley cats, with immense satisfaction. Lord John had risen politely when the viscount was announced, but that was as far as his cordiality extended. The animosity between the two men was apparent and their civil greetings did little to disguise it. She rubbed her plump hands in anticipation.

Lord John possessed the advantage of having the chair between Miss Talbot and her kind-hearted mama; Lord Brownlow, arriving a few minutes later, was forced to seat himself to the right of Lady Throckmorton. The chair was scarcely comfortable—having a hard, straight back—uncommonly warm—being closest to the fire—and precariously placed in front of yet another dog sprawled on the rug. He seated himself awkwardly, trying to find a place for his long legs without disturbing the pug which had opened one eye and emitted a low growl.

Had it been any other gentleman, Johnny would have felt a measure of sympathy. For Lord Brownlow, there was none. His eyes took in the viscount's impeccably tailored attire, which he had little trouble in recognising as a product of France. After noting the ladies' admiring glances, he hoped very much that the pug might be induced to take a healthy bite out of Brownlow's tightly clad legs.

Feeling the heated glance, the viscount looked up, his smile vastly superior. "I trust you are quite recovered from your travels, my lord? You appear much improved since our last meeting."

Diana bit her lip. It was a low thrust and ill-mannered of Lord Brownlow to remind Lord John of his recent malady. She quickly pressed cups of tea on both gentlemen.

"Quite," Johnny replied, accepting the cup but with his gaze still focussed on Brownlow. He added, "The journey to Town was a trifle difficult, however, and I was forced to overnight at Allington."

"Oh? Do carriages make you ill, as well?" Brownlow asked with mock sympathy.

"Not at all. The delay was due to a gentleman I found lying in the road. He had been cruelly shot and left without help. I believe you are all acquainted with him: Lieutenant Jennot."

"Jennot? Are you referring to that officious French lieutenant who detained us in St. Omer?" Lady Throckmorton demanded, her double chins quivering with remembered indignation.

Diana's hands trembled on her teacup and she quickly set it down on the table near her chair, her eyes on Johnny as she waited for him to reply.

"The same," he acknowledged, and deliberately paused, sipping his tea. He had all their attention now. The three ladies showed considerable astonishment, and demanded explanations, but Brownlow merely narrowed his eyes and waited silently for him to continue.

"I chanced upon him where you left him in the road," Johnny continued as though he were discussing some mundane trifle left behind. "Oh, yes, he knew it was you, my lord. Indeed, he believes you recognised him, and is rather puzzled by your haste in putting a bullet in him. Had I not interfered, the poor fellow would have died."

"Am I to shed crocodile tears?" Brownlow sneered. "French lieutenant or not, he had no business stopping a private coach in England. I assumed, as anyone naturally would, that he was a footpad and acted to safeguard the ladies."

"How strange, for he swore you recognised him," Johnny murmured. "Might I have more tea, Miss Talbot?"

She refilled his cup with shaking hands, remembering all too clearly Jennot's vow to capture the Black Domino. Was that why Lord Brownlow had shot him and left him to die? *Had* he recognised the lieutenant?

Her fingers touched Johnny's as she passed him the cup, and she glanced up to see his blue eyes, full of concern, watching her closely, and knew she must not appear so agitated. She managed a tremulous smile. "This is most distressing, sir. I gather the lieutenant has recovered?"

He nodded. "He seemed well on the mend when I left him, but as I said, is most displeased with our friend here."

She could not help contrasting Lord John's air of calm civility with that of the viscount, whose florid face wore a hard and unbecoming look of angry disdain. Did she not know the true reason, she would think Lord Brownlow most cold. The notion disturbed her and she reminded herself that it was merely a mask he wore to protect his true identity.

"Thank heaven for that," Violet Talbot uttered distractedly as she searched in her reticule for her smelling salts. "It would have been quite dreadful had he died. I mean, someone we *knew*—" she broke off uncertainly, perceiving the viscount was not pleased.

"Regrettable, perhaps," Lady Throckmorton pronounced, judging it time she intervened. "But Lord Brownlow is in the right of it. The lieutenant had no business stopping our carriage, and if he was wounded in the process, he has only his own impertinence to blame. I wish to hear no more of this. Yes, James, what is it?"

The footman stood hesitantly just inside the door. "Lord Claypool is calling, my lady—"

"What the devil is *he* doing here?" she interrupted rudely, disturbing one of the pugs on her lap.

"I invited him, Mother," Violet said, a trifle flustered. "I did not think you would object."

Lady Throckmorton opened her lips to denounce her daughter as a stupid fool incapable of rational thought, but abruptly changed her mind. Perhaps Violet had some notion of showing Brownlow he was not the only suitor for Diana's hand. It might be foolish, but it could not hurt. She nodded grudgingly to the footman. "Show him in, James."

Diana, blushing at the mention of the gentleman's name, wished fervently that her mama would not be so obvious in her efforts to get her married off. She busied herself with the tea service, and missed the look of pleasure on her mother's face when Lord Claypool entered the room.

He moved lightly for a man of his girth and crossed the floor to bow before Lady Throckmorton, as was her due. He thrust a bouquet of wild flowers awkwardly into Mrs. Talbot's hands, murmured that Diana was looking charming as ever, nodded to Brownlow and turned to Johnny with patent relief.

"Didn't expect to find such a crowd here," he said, settling his huge bulk in the chair James drew up by Mrs. Talbot.

"If you will excuse me, I shall just put these in some water," Violet said, rising. "They are quite beautiful, Lord Claypool."

The gentlemen rose at once.

"Must you make such a fuss, Violet? Give them to Simmonds. She can put them in Diana's room," Lady Throckmorton ordered.

Violet turned a bright shade of pink and Claypool coughed. "Daresay you can't be faulted for thinking Miss Talbot is the only one in the house to receive posies, but those are for her mama." Oblivious to Lady Throckmorton's wide-eyed astonishment, he smiled gently at Violet. "Thought they might cheer you up a trifle on such a dismal day."

"Thank you, my lord," she whispered and fled with her flowers before her mother could object further.

The gentlemen remained standing, waiting for her return, and Lord Claypool, thinking only to divert the conversation, turned to Brownlow. "Not surprised to see you here, my lord," he joked, with a broad wink. "Word's out all over Town you mean to have—" He broke off as the viscount stared at him, plainly annoyed. "That is to say, er, well, I wish you better luck than me."

Lady Throckmorton raised her quizzing glass and stared at him, for once struck speechless, and wondering if Claypool had completely lost his wits. Diana did not know where to look, and sat motionless, silently wishing she could sink through the floor.

"I should not wager on it," Johnny said, his words an icy warning as he met Brownlow's eyes.

One of the pugs raised its fat neck and growled menacingly. Lady Throckmorton laid a plump hand on its head. The visit was not progressing at all as she had envisaged. "Quiet, Dulcie," she ordered. "As for you gentlemen, I will thank you to remember that you are in a drawing-room. If you cannot conduct yourselves accordingly, you have my permission to withdraw."

Neither Lord John nor Lord Brownlow was willing to leave the field to the other, and though both nodded in response, Lady Throckmorton's pronouncement did little to lessen the strain between them.

Lord Claypool, realising his blunder, coloured, mentally cursed his unruly tongue and would have fled at once had not Violet chosen that moment to return. He greeted her thankfully and the tension was temporarily eased as they resumed their seats.

Diana, seeking desperately to turn the conversation, addressed Lord John. "Pray tell me, sir, how is our poor little orphan faring? Is your brother willing to offer the boy employment?"

Willing was perhaps not the appropriate word to describe his brother's reaction to Alfie, but Johnny nodded. "For the moment, but if Alfie continues to set the house on end, I cannot promise you Spence won't give him the boot."

"Oh, dear. I had hoped—he looked like such a nice boy. Has he done something quite dreadful?" Diana asked, concerned.

"Well, you should not be in the least surprised," Lady Throckmorton said testily. "I warned you, did I not? One cannot take a base-born brat and put him in a gentleman's house without expecting dire consequences."

"There was no great harm done, and it was hardly the boy's fault," Johnny said and, with the air of a conspirator, smiled warmly at Diana. "While the footmen were giving the lad a bath yesterday, his pup escaped the confines of the kitchen and ran afoul of my brother's prize spaniel. There was a mad chase down the hall, and they knocked over a pedestal with a vase of flowers just as my brother stepped in the door. Unfortunately, betwixt the water on the floor and the dogs beneath his heels, Spencer tripped and ended up sitting on his dignity."

Diana's mouth curved up at the corners as she imagined the scene, and her eyes met Johnny's in shared amusement.

"My stars! I hope his lordship was not injured," Violet Talbot murmured. "He must have been most astonished."

"Not the sort of welcome a gentleman looks for," Lord Claypool added, "but I must say it was good of you to take the child in. Mrs. Talbot told me what occurred."

Brownlow, feeling decidedly *de trop,* set down his cup. "I don't know how you came by an orphan, but I must agree with Lady Throckmorton. It never answers to take children out of their natural environment."

"Lord John rescued him yesterday," Diana replied, a shade of reproach in her low voice. "He was nearly run down by a herd of cattle. If you had but seen the poor child, I believe your heart must have been touched."

"Do not misunderstand me, Miss Talbot. I abhor the plight of the orphans, as any gentleman of feeling must, but bringing them into your own home, my dear, is not the answer. Such an arrangement leaves them awkward and ill at ease, and can only have, as Lady Throckmorton so rightly pointed out, disastrous results."

"I disagree, my lord," Johnny said before Diana could answer. "We are all mortals composed of mere blood and bone. It is only opportunity that sets us apart from less fortunate souls.''

"Poppycock!" Lady Throckmorton declared firmly. "What utter fustian! Breeding will always tell, young man. It is true in dogs and horses, and you'll find it the same with people," she said, fondling the head of one of her pugs. "I doubt you would wager so much as a shilling on a horse did you not first inspect his blood lines!''

Violet blushed at such frank discussion in front of her unwed daughter, but Diana was following the conversation with interest.

"True, my lady, and yet some very promising foals have proved disappointing when put to the test. The same can be said of certain well-bred gentlemen, men provided with every possible advantage, who have inexplicably turned out to be... dirty dishes,'' Johnny said, looking directly at the viscount.

There was no mistaking his meaning, and Brownlow's face flushed an angry red. His fingers curled into a fist and he half rose.

"That's so," Claypool muttered, stepping unwittingly into the fray. "Only look at poor old King George, mad as a hatter, for all his blue blood. And Princess Caroline. No one can say she is a lady born,'' he added, with a loud chuckle.

An ominous quiet greeted his sally and he became unpleasantly aware of the scowl on Lady Throckmorton's face, and the derision in Lord Brownlow's eyes. Mrs. Talbot seemed abnormally intent on tracing the embroidered lines of her skirt. He thought he caught a flash of amusement in Diana's eyes, but she quickly ducked her head.

Only Lord John seemed at ease. He rose with languid grace and made a bow in Lady Throckmorton's direction, his expressive eyes fairly dancing with laughter. "I fear I have overstayed my welcome, my lady, and must beg your pardon."

"Impertinent jackanapes. Take yourself off before I forget I was bred a lady and tell you what I think of your base-born manners!"

"Mother!" Violet cried, shocked.

Johnny saw the amusement in the old woman's eyes and grinned unabashedly. "Your most obedient servant, madam."

DIANA HAD AMPLE opportunity to reflect on the idiocy of inviting two gentlemen of irreparably different tastes to call on the same day. She later described it to Venetia Courtland as quite the longest afternoon she had ever endured, and the only redeeming value was the knowledge she'd gleaned of her mother's growing attachment to Lord Claypool, which, it seemed, was warmly returned. Diana had teased her mother unmercifully for "cutting her out," at which Violet blushed prettily, begged her not to use vulgar slang, and declaimed. But the truth could not be denied, and when the knocker was heard in the ensuing days, it was Lord Claypool arriving for tea, or seeking to take Mrs. Talbot for an afternoon drive or a stroll through the park.

Diana was not unduly concerned when Lord Brownlow did not call; he had told her he would be engaged with pressing business affairs for several days. Lord John, however, had promised to keep her apprised of the progress of their orphan, and she was more than a little disappointed when he failed to call, and looked for him in vain at two evening parties she attended.

Venetia was less than understanding and would only remark that she had warned Diana how it would be.

When Lord Brownlow had refused Tom's invitation to dine on the grounds of prior business engagements, Venetia had reluctantly agreed to ask Lord John. But he, too, had declined, and she remarked to Diana that there must be a rash of urgent business being conducted in London to preoccupy so many gentlemen. She apologised for seating her friend with prosy Edward Hibbert, but he was the only unattached male of her acquaintance available on such short notice.

Venetia's dinner, by most standards, was considered a success, and if Diana found it rather dull, she knew it was her own *ennui* to blame and she returned home in a chastened mood. She sought out her mother, thinking to have a comfortable chat before retiring, only to be informed by Annie that Mrs. Talbot was out for the evening with Lord Claypool, and not expected to return until late. Her grandmother had also retired, along with her pugs, and Diana was left with her own melancholy reflections.

She retired early to bed but found herself unable to sleep. She tried to focus her mind on Lord Brownlow and his rather heroic deeds as the Black Domino. Was it really true, she wondered, that familiarity breeds contempt? Not that she held him in contempt . . . it was only that now and then he disappointed her in little things. His attitude over the orphan boy was but one example. And yet, it was an opinion shared by many gentlemen, and she supposed he could not be faulted for that. Surely, she did not want him to behave like Lord John. Madcap Johnny, she thought, smiling, and wished again that he would call.

Restlessly, she turned over and repositioned her pillow. She told herself her desire to see Lord John was only due to her interest in the orphan. After all, she rea-

soned, she'd had a hand in rescuing the child and it was
only natural that she be curious as to his welfare. But for
all his faults and his idle existence, she had to admit she
did admire Lord John . . . just a little. She had no trouble
recalling the way his blue eyes seemed to sparkle when he
was amused, and the rakish way his dark hair curled
down over his brow. . . . This would not do, she told herself sternly. Whatever was she thinking of! Madcap
Johnny was *not* the sort of gentleman she admired. Not
really.

Matters improved slightly on Friday when Lord
Brownlow appeared and enquired if he might take her
driving. Diana willingly agreed and spent a pleasant hour
in his company in Hyde Park, much in charity with him.
He was once again impeccably dressed—not at all in the
careless style Lord John affected—and his skill with a
team was impressive. She sat quietly beside him, admiring his prowess, and listening as he described some of the
pleasures of living abroad.

She hoped he might request the privilege of escorting
her to Lady Jersey's masquerade ball that evening, an
event already much discussed and likely to be the most
successful of the Season, but when they neared Manchester Square, he still had not broached the matter. Diana,
unaccustomed to angling for escorts, hesitantly mentioned that she had found an exceptionally fine domino,
a dark blue cape and hood aglitter with paste jewels, that
she planned to wear that evening to Lady Jersey's.

"I wish I might see you," he remarked, handing her
down from the carriage, "but I doubt I shall be free in
time."

Her disappointment was hard to mask, and she quickly
lowered her head.

The viscount placed a gloved hand beneath her chin and tilted her face up. "Diana, I wish I might court you in the style you deserve. Unfortunately, I have not the freedom of other gentlemen. There are concerns which—"

"I understand," she interrupted softly. "If I am disappointed, it is only for the moment. I would not for the world have you neglect your duties. What you do is far more important than a silly ball."

Lord Brownlow hid his astonishment at so easy an acceptance. If Miss Talbot knew his pressing business was a high-stakes macao game, no doubt she'd not be quite so forgiving. But it hardly mattered. Had he nothing at all to do, he still could not attend the masquerade ball. Sally Jersey was a high stickler and several years ago had cut him directly. It was highly unlikely she would ever extend him an invitation, but no point in telling Diana that. He smiled tenderly down at her. "Thank you, my dear, for being so understanding. I promise you, if it is at all possible, I shall try to look in for a few moments late this evening."

With that Diana had to be content. It was difficult, for she had to bear the sarcastic barbs of Lady Throckmorton on her lack of suitors, and harder still, the kind sympathy of her mother. Still, Diana had Lord Brownlow's promise to comfort her and the secret knowledge that he was engaged on important affairs of state. It became increasingly hard to keep such idealistic thoughts in mind, however, as she passed through the receiving line at Lady Jersey's and into the ballroom, trailing after her mother and Lord Claypool.

The Grand Ballroom was aglow with hundreds of tiny lights. Lady Jersey had created an enchanted woodland by bringing in masses of huge potted plants and filling their branches with tiny candles. Additional mirrors adorned the walls, reflecting the lights and festooned with long lengths of satiny gold and silver ribbons. The effect was breathtaking, and the soft lilting sounds of the orchestra beckoned.

Diana was approached almost at once by a masked Centurion who begged the pleasure of a dance. She nodded, thinking she recognised George Sewell beneath the black mask, but she preferred not to know for certain. It was much more exciting to be swept away by a stranger. Her Centurion gave way to a Gladiator, and later a handsome pirate partnered her in one of the country dances. She counted at least three gentlemen dressed like the Duke of Wellington and one who pretended he was Napoleon just escaped, and she laughed at his atrocious French accent. The majority of gentlemen, however, wore their usual evening dress and disguised themselves only by means of colourful masks.

The evening was passing more pleasurably than she had anticipated, though neither Lord Brownlow or Lord John had put in an appearance. Her slippered feet ached from so much dancing, and the last gentleman had carelessly trod upon her toes. She thought she would seek out her mama and discover how much longer they meant to remain. But it was exceedingly difficult to discover one person among such a crush, and the room was growing increasingly stuffy. Diana moved near the open terrace door to catch a hint of the cooling breeze. She was standing there alone, shortly before midnight, when a tall gentleman came up behind her and whispered softly in her ear.

"Good evening, Miss Talbot."

She whirled about, thinking she recognised the low, husky voice, and looked up searchingly into a pair of amused blue eyes, barely visible behind a tight-fitting black mask. It was cleverly tied to the hood of the domino and concealed all but the gentleman's brow, lips and firm chin. She had seen only one other mask like it and wondered if it were indeed the same.

He bowed before her and when he straightened he produced a long-stemmed, delicately fashioned black silk rose.

Diana stared at it, entranced.

"Have you forgotten my promise, then?" he asked, his deep voice full of teasing. His hand moved, bringing the tip of the rose to brush gently against her mouth.

Her hand closed over his. "It is you, then!"

"Come to claim the lady of my heart," he whispered, encircling her tiny waist with his other hand.

She moved as though she were in a dream, allowing the Domino to draw her into his arms. The clasp of his hand against her back and the strength of his arms felt hauntingly familiar. Even without the rose, she would have been positive of his identity and did not object when he guided her through the open terrace door.

For several minutes they waltzed on the dimly lit balcony without speaking. It was enough to be in his arms again. She felt the same thrill of excitement that had stirred her in Dover and did not object when the gentleman continued to hold her close after the music had stopped.

"I can stay for only a few moments, dearest."

"I am surprised you were able to come at all," she answered softly. "And pleased to see you for even so brief a time."

"Remember that, and do not worry should you not see me for a week or two. I promise I will return to you as soon as I may and claim you for my own. This is to be my last journey."

"You are going back to France," she said, suddenly chilled. "Oh, promise me you will be careful."

"Diana, sweet Diana," he murmured, touched by her concern. "I have never met another... not with brown eyes so lustrous or skin as soft as a rose...." he said, before bending his head to brush her lips.

She lifted her mouth to his eagerly, thrilled that he had remembered the words he'd whispered in Dover. He had never mentioned them again, and she thought at times that perhaps she had imagined the entire interlude. But his kiss was real. There could be no doubting that or the way it made her heart race. She felt the muscles of his arms harden as he pulled her yet closer, and still it was not close enough. Her arms tightened about his neck....

She was released abruptly, and the Domino pulled her into a darkened corner, whispering a warning. "Hush, I hear someone coming."

Then she heard the high-pitched voice of her cousin Emily. "I am positive I saw her come out here, Horace! It is my duty to make sure she comes to no harm."

Diana realised the predicament she was in. If Emily caught her alone on the balcony with a gentleman, her cousin could be counted on to create a scene that would draw the attention of everyone within shouting distance. And they were fairly trapped behind a large potted shrub!

The Domino drew her protectively against him, his hands caressing her arms while he whispered against her hair. "I loathe leaving you so soon, but remember my promise. The next time I present you with a black rose, I will claim you openly. Wait for me, Diana." He kissed her brow lightly and then turned and vaulted over side of the balcony. Diana peered over the edge, her eyes straining for a glimpse of him, but there was only a thin crescent moon that did little to alter the pitch black of the night.

"You must have been mistaken, my dear."

"I tell you, Horace, I saw her. She must be out here somewhere—there is only the one door."

Diana listened for a moment and then coughed softly.

"There! What did I tell you?" Emily crowed and hurried towards the dark corner. "Diana? Are you out here, cousin?"

"Are you looking for me, Emily?" Diana asked sweetly. "I was just standing here admiring the beauty of the night. It is lovely, is it not?" she asked, leaning against the wrought-iron balcony. "But perhaps it is a trifle cool for you? Mr. Bottomham, do you think she ought to be out here, in her condition?"

"Perhaps you are right," he conceded while his wife edged round to peer behind the shrub.

Search as she might, there was no place a gentleman could be concealed, and Emily looked at her cousin in confusion. "But you are alone," she wailed in considerable disappointment.

CHAPTER NINE

"You look out of reason content for a miss who spent the evening chaperoning her mama," Lady Throckmorton commented crossly at the breakfast table the following morning.

"Hardly that," Violet protested, looking fondly at her daughter. "I daresay Diana did not sit out one dance last evening."

"Which shows how unobservant you are, Violet. I have it on good authority that your daughter spent at least part of the evening on the balcony. Alone."

"Oh, has Cousin Emily already called this morning?" Diana asked with mock sweetness. "How very thoughtful of her to take such interest in my affairs, but I do hope she was not too terribly disappointed at finding me alone last night? I should so hate to distress her when she is in such a delicate condition," she added, pushing her plate aside and reaching for the mail.

"You have a nasty tongue in your head, my girl, and I would advise you to guard it carefully. I see no suitors knocking on the door, and if this is an example of how you mean to squander your time in London, we may as well remove to Bath."

"If you are referring to Lord Brownlow's absence, I believe I mentioned he is occupied with pressing business concerns, Grandmama. Indeed, he regretted that he would be unable to see me for the next week or two,"

Diana replied calmly and continued sorting the stack of invitations and letters.

"Hmmph. Next, I suppose you will be telling me that Lord John is too busy attending to *his* business affairs to call!"

"I have no notion of what Lord John may be doing, nor do I care," Diana said, but feared the blush colouring her cheeks would betray her. Hoping to distract her grandmother, she passed across several letters and handed a smaller stack to her mother.

"Just as well," her grandmother remarked, watching her closely. "I doubt you could bring him up to scratch."

"This is most odd," Violet said suddenly, examining a creamy linen envelope. "The Countess of Granville has written to me. I do not believe I have ever met the lady. I wonder what she could possibly..."

"Oh, for heaven's sake, open the letter," Lady Throckmorton ordered impatiently.

Violet obeyed her and quickly scanned the neatly penned lines. "How exceedingly thoughtful of her," she murmured after a moment.

"What is it, Mama?" Diana asked, unable to contain her own curiosity any longer.

"She invites both of us to dine tomorrow—just a small, informal affair. But she writes that she has requested Lord Claypool's company, as well, and if it is agreeable to me, he could provide us escort. Otherwise, she will be pleased to send her carriage."

"A sensible young woman," Lady Throckmorton pronounced. "And no doubt she heard how you made a cake of yourself last night, hanging on Lord Claypool's arm all evening."

It was Violet's turn to blush, and Diana immediately came to her mother's defence. "My cousin has been a great deal too busy! If anyone made a cake of herself, it was Emily—dragging her poor husband out on the balcony and searching all the corners for some imaginary gentleman," she said, anger sharpening her voice. Oblivious to the astonished stares of the footmen, she pushed back her chair and rose. "My dear cousin very nearly created a scene and had it not been for Bottomham's calm good sense in removing her, I fear all London would be talking this morning of poor mad Emily. Obviously, her condition has made her prone to delusions," she added, and then swept from the room before her grandmother could protest.

Diana hurried up to her bedchamber. She was instantly sorry for her outburst and intended to apologise when she sufficiently calmed her nerves. She paced the room, wondering at her agitation. It was not like her to respond to her grandmother's needling so violently and she owned that, in part, it was her own guilt at nearly being caught out by her cousin that was setting her on edge. It had been foolhardy to step out on the balcony with the Domino... and yet, such was his spell over her that she knew she would do it again.

There had been times during the past month when she wondered if she'd been mistaken in her affections. Times when she'd been unreasonably disappointed in Lord Brownlow, and feared perhaps her hero had feet of clay. But any doubts she'd had about her growing love for that gentleman had been effectively erased by his kisses. There was something indisputably right about the way she'd felt in his arms—a sort of homecoming, and she knew with every one of her senses that this was where she belonged.

She smiled at such fanciful thoughts and picked up the silk rose from her dressing table, remembering his promise anew. Her fingers absently stroked the delicate black petals, and she wished everything were settled between them. She suffered no doubts or worries when she was nestled in the reassuring strength of his arms. She reminded herself he'd promised to return in a fortnight. Surely, she thought, she could be patient until then. She had waited for him for years—what was another week or two? But waiting was proving unbearable, especially now that she knew he was in danger.

IT WOULD HAVE PERHAPS soothed Diana to know that the Black Domino was equally impatient to settle his affairs, and equally agitated. He left the Duke of Cardiff's Town house with a sense of impending doom. First, his departure for France had been postponed for two days, and however much he dreaded the trip, he wanted it over and done with. But what disturbed him most was the news of a new plan afoot to rescue the prisoner.

The duke's agent reported that a certain captain of the French Guard had suffered heavy gambling debts and was not averse to accepting a substantial bribe. The captain was willing to look the other way while Monsieur Rousseau was spirited out of the palace at Versailles, and he had even provided a key to the condemned man's cell. The hair on the back of Johnny's neck had risen when he heard the ease with which the escape was being planned. It was too providential.

The duke agreed the captain could probably not be trusted, but his co-operation made getting Jean-Baptiste Rousseau out of the palace the least of their difficulties. The place crawled with foreign visitors, and tradesmen of all sorts were permitted in every part of the palace. It would be a simple matter to disguise three of his men among such a horde. The real problem, he said, was a

recent dispatch indicating Jean-Baptiste was terribly ill.
It could make travelling with him difficult, and no matter how much the captain was bribed, he was certain to
sound an alarm once Rousseau was clear of the palace.
A hue and cry would be raised and a massive hunt
launched. That was where Johnny was needed.

"They will be expecting Rousseau to make for Le
Havre and sail from there to Portsmouth. It is undoubtedly the fastest route, and therefore will be the most
heavily guarded. You, my friend, will be waiting north of
Versailles, in Mantes, where Rousseau will be delivered
into your hands. If you can get him to Dieppe, I shall
have a yacht waiting there to bring you both across and
into Brighton."

"It has the stench of a trap," Johnny pointed out with
a marked lack of enthusiasm.

The duke nodded. "More than likely, but we can ill
afford to turn down the opportunity. Without the captain's help—" He broke off, shrugging. "I hope we can
turn the trap to our own advantage, and for that, I am
counting on you."

What worried Johnny most was hearing Cardiff's final, chilling words. Words as cold as his eyes. "Rousseau must not be left in France alive, John. The lives of
dozens of our men depend on it. I pray you will succeed
in bringing him out, but if not...you understand me, do
you not, John?"

He understood all too well and he left the house with
the duke's orders hanging over him like a heavy grey fog.
He drove mindlessly, failing to return a salute from Tom
Courtland as their carriages passed, and never saw
George Somerset waving at him from the street.

For years he had delighted in outwitting the French,
pulling off the most extravagant and outrageous of ex-

ploits beneath Napoleon's nose. It was a game of cat and mouse and he had thrilled to the danger, willingly risking his life on behalf of his country. He had taken pride in the growing reputation of the Black Domino. Now, with the little Corsican safe on St. Helena and the war ended, it all seemed a pointless waste. Too many good men were dying. Johnny sighed. He was tired of the duplicity of politicians—duplicity that placed the lives of men like Jennot and Rousseau at risk. Would their countries never learn to live in peace?

Old habits die hard, and though he could not confide in Spencer, Johnny sought the solace of his brother's company. He surrendered his hat and cap to Hadley with none of his usual insouciance, and quietly followed the butler to the drawing-room. Juliana greeted him warmly, as usual, but he was unreasonably disappointed not to find Spencer at home and responded to her teasing with only a polite show of humour until she finally took him to task.

"Johnny, what is amiss? I have never seen you look so downcast. Are you in trouble of some sort?"

That brought a ghost of a smile to his lips. "No, just a bit blue-deviled. Pay me no mind."

"Well, I hope it will improve your spirits to know that Miss Talbot and her mama have accepted an invitation to dine with us tomorrow," she said, and then laughed as he looked decidedly more cheerful. "Yes, I rather thought it might."

He grinned and reached out a hand, capturing hers and bringing it to his lips for a chaste kiss. "The notion of dining with you would always cheer me, my dear. Have I told you how very becoming that gown is? The green enhances the pretty colour of your eyes."

"Shameless boy! Go and amuse your nephew while I speak to Cook for a few minutes. John Louis is in the nursery with Poppy," she said, rising. He looked puzzled and she added, "You do recall the girl you sent to Crowley from Dover? She arrived here a few days ago and, Johnny, she has been a positive Godsend. I cannot thank you enough for sending her to me. She is simply wonderful and the baby absolutely adores her. Even Spencer is pleased to approve."

He smiled at the last and made his way to the nursery. Poppy was almost as delighted as John Louis to see him, and tried to express her gratitude again. He waved away her effusive thanks, though he felt a small measure of satisfaction at seeing her looking much better. Her blond hair was neatly combed, her dress clean and starched, and the thin, pinched look was gone from her glowing eyes. At least he had done one thing right. It was a pity, he thought, that he could not set his own life in order as neatly as he had arranged Poppy's.

THE EARL OF GRANVILLE was considerably startled the following evening when his scapegrace younger brother not only arrived early, but rather somberly clad. He whispered to Juliana that it was difficult to believe it was the madcap, and enquired with mock solemnity if there had been a death in the family.

She hushed him, and was at pains to tell Johnny how handsome he looked, which was no more than the truth. She noted with some surprise that the elegant black evening coat, with its high velvet collar suited him, as did the tight-fitting black pantaloons. It was just that one was accustomed to seeing him more brightly garbed, and not quite so stern of demeanour. However, he was not in the house above five minutes, when two errant curls escaped his efforts at a neat coiffure and fell across his brow, quite destroying his air of sobriety.

Johnny accepted the glass of sherry his brother offered, enquired politely as to his health and otherwise waited impatiently for the arrival of Miss Talbot.

Juliana, watching his eyes continuously straying to the clock on the mantelpiece, and the eager way he turned every time the door opened, began to suspect that Miss Talbot was a force to be reckoned with. Her suspicion was confirmed when Hadley announced the arrival of their guests. Juliana knew Johnny had once fancied himself in love with her, but he had *never* looked at her the way he was looking at Diana Talbot. She prayed the girl was as sweet-natured as she was beautiful, and crossed the room to welcome the Talbots and Lord Claypool.

Diana had taken pains to be at her best that evening, telling herself it was because of the earl and her hopes of persuading him to speak in the House of Lords on behalf of the orphans. It was for that reason that she had worn her new gown. She recalled the charming remarks of the modiste when she'd tried it on. Madam had said the deep gold tones of the half robe set off sparks in her chestnut hair and brought out the hazel in her eyes, while the soft cream-coloured slip beneath accented her delicate complexion and heightened the natural colour in her cheeks.

Diana had privately thought it an exaggeration—no doubt prompted by the size of madam's commission—but there was no denying the look of admiration in Lord John's eyes as he took her hand. One could not help but be flattered by such warm approval, she thought, feeling the tingle that passed through her fingers and up her arm. It was only when she looked away from the mesmerising blue eyes that she realised she'd allowed him to hold her hand for much too long and that they were the cynosure of all eyes.

Diana stepped hastily away from him and made it a point to keep her attention focussed on the earl and the countess. Lord Granville was not nearly as intimidating as she'd been led to believe. He welcomed her warmly, at pains to set her at ease. She caught the glint of humour in his eyes as they spoke, and wondered if he had been as engaging a youth as Lord John. Almost against her will, her gaze was drawn to where Johnny sat, making idle conversation with her mother.

"Is your acquaintance with my brother of long standing, Miss Talbot?" Spencer asked, politely recalling her attention.

Diana flushed, feeling much like a child caught coveting some treat, and endeavoured to answer composedly. "Not very long, my lord. We met only this Season...."

"I see, and yet I am told you are the young lady responsible for persuading Johnny to introduce an orphan into my household."

She looked up then and saw his generous smile and the warmth in his eyes and relaxed slightly. "I do apologise, my lord, for the trouble he caused. Lord John told me of your... your encounter with the child."

Spencer laughed softly. "How kind of you to phrase it so politely, my dear, but do not apologise. Had it not been this boy, I fear it would have been some other. Both my wife and my brother seem to have a propensity for adopting strays—of all sorts. Alfie is not the first, and will likely not be the last."

"Lord John?" she asked, astonished, and glanced at him again. "I had not realised he—" She broke off abruptly, realising how rude her remark might be considered.

The earl smiled, perfectly understanding her. "Few people do. I fear John's reputation as a madcap is talked of far more than his good deeds. Indeed, it is often his soft heart that leads him into his more bizarre escapades."

Johnny, making polite conversation across the room with Basil and Mrs. Talbot, glanced frequently at the pair near the fireplace and wondered what Spence could be saying to make Diana laugh in just that way. He felt a twinge of jealousy and was the first to rise when Hadley finally appeared and announced dinner.

They dined informally in the small parlour. Spencer sat at the head of the table with Juliana at the opposite end. Diana was placed between the earl and Johnny, and Mrs. Talbot and Lord Claypool were seated across from them. With such a small gathering, the countess declared there would be no formality and conversation across the table was permitted.

The earl was at his diplomatic best. At the onset, Diana was inclined to be serious and spoke passionately of the plight of the orphans—which, she reminded herself, was the reason she had accepted the invitation to dinner. She was surprised to learn her host was not only a patron but a Governor of the Foundling Hospital, and that a number of his personal staff had come from the orphanage. The earl won her instant approval when he told her of bills he hoped to introduce to expand the facilities to accommodate more children.

She praised his efforts warmly, but Spencer shrugged it off.

"Self-preservation, my dear. Something must be done before my home is utterly destroyed. Many more lads like

Alfie and I fear it is I who will be seeking shelter. Did Johnny tell you that boy nearly set the library on fire?"

"You exaggerate, Spence," Johnny interrupted. "It was only the tiniest of flames, and you have to admit he stamped it out at once."

"Oh, I do, and that intriguing burn in the Aubusson carpet must surely be held to add to its design. But you mistake me, John. I scarcely hold the child to blame," his brother said with a wry smile. "As I recall, it was you who brought that infernal device back from France. What is it called? Oh, yes. The Instantaneous Light Box. Just the thing to attract the attention of a lad like Alfie."

Mrs. Talbot smothered a laugh and Basil chuckled aloud.

Johnny, not at all chastened, grinned impudently. "Any person with a curious mind would naturally be interested in such a device. I only wonder you were so careless as to leave it lying about."

"Had I known my household was suddenly going to include a boy as incorrigible as your orphan, I assure you it would have been under lock and key," Spencer said, and added with mock severity, "He rather reminds me of you at his age. Indeed, I suspect your affinity for the boy is due to your being so much alike."

How delightful this is, Diana thought, listening to the banter between the brothers. She glanced round the table, comparing it to the disquieting meals she frequently shared with her mother and grandmother. She could not recall when she had been so amused, or seen her mother quite as happy. Neither the earl nor Juliana, as she insisted she be called, could have been more kind. And Lord John had a quick wit she had not suspected. She looked up to find him watching her and something about the amusement in his blue eyes startled her, reminding her uncomfortably of another gentleman. She realised with no little astonishment that she had not given Lord Brownlow a thought the entire evening.

"Now, what has caused that frown between your pretty brows?" Johnny whispered as a footman passed round the table removing their plates.

"It is nothing," she murmured, but kept her eyes down.

Juliana saw her distress and rose. "I believe it is time we ladies withdrew and allowed you gentlemen to enjoy your port and cigars. If you will excuse us?"

The three men rose at once and remained standing while the countess led her guests to the salon. It was an elegant apartment, with its high ceiling and lavish scroll-work. The wall of stained-glass windows was held to be one of the finest in all of London, but unfortunately the panes did not seem to fit well into the casements and constant drafts kept the room noticeably chilly.

The ladies seated themselves comfortably about the fireplace, thankful for its warmth, and Juliana re-marked tactfully, "I fear my husband sometimes must give a false impression, the way he teases Johnny, but in truth he dotes on his brother. Did you know, my dear, that they were orphaned at an early age?"

Diana admitted her surprise but added, "It is easy to see how fond they are of each other. I sometimes wish I had a sister...."

"Then we have that in common. I, too, am an only child, and enjoy the closeness of my husband's family."

"It is, indeed, most pleasant to sit down with such a congenial family," Mrs. Talbot said, a trace of envy in her voice. "If the rest of the earl's relations are as cordial, you are extremely fortunate, my lady."

"Thank you," Juliana said with one of her warm smiles. "I do consider myself blessed." She turned to Diana, curiosity overriding her manners. "I believe you are acquainted with Johnny's Aunt Georgia, Lady Guilford?"

"I have met the lady," Diana owned hesitantly. "Though I had no notion she was Johnny's aunt." She recalled the rather delicate blond beauty whom she'd encountered on a few social occasions. "It is hard to imagine her in such a household as this. She seems rather aloof...or perhaps that is merely her manner with strangers?"

Juliana laughed at the notion of Georgia holding herself aloof. "I promise you, she is the most warm-hearted of creatures. If she appears otherwise to you, I fear it is only that she believes you disapprove of her."

"I? Why on earth should she think so?" Diana asked, truly astonished. "I would never be so presumptuous!"

Juliana took her hand in her own. "It is all a misunderstanding, I believe." She explained Georgia's tale of embarrassment at being caught in the garden with the Duke of Clarence, adding, "And so you see, she has been a trifle embarrassed every time you chanced to meet."

"Oh, my heavens! You must believe I did not see her, though I recall that evening. I stepped out into the gardens to escape the attentions of Lord Uxbridge. He had been pursuing me for several days and I was at a loss to know how to deal with him. My grandmother rather thought I should welcome his attentions, but I—I could not."

"Uxbridge! Pardon me, my dear, but I wonder at Lady Throckmorton's encouraging him. I have seldom met a more rude or obnoxious creature."

"Nor I," Diana said with an answering smile. "But you must understand that he behaved like a perfect gentleman in front of Grandmama, and she has always been anxious to see me marry well."

"But Uxbridge—oh, I am sorry, do go on."

Diana shrugged. "There is not much more to tell. I thought he had retired to the billiard room and that I was safe in stepping outside for a breath of air. He followed me, of course, and tried to kiss me." She shivered, recalling the man's foul breath and wet, sloppy mouth. "It was the first time a gentleman had ever made improper advances to me, and I fear I was so shocked that I'd no notion of what I was about. All I could think of was to get away from him. I ran into the salon—it was mortifying the way everyone suddenly seemed to be staring, and I suppose I must have presented an odd appearance. I fled the room and ran up to my bedchamber."

"It is a pity you were not better acquainted with Georgia. Had she known your problem, she would have sent Uxbridge off with a flea in his ear. Only wait until you hear some of her maxims for dealing with gentlemen," Juliana told her.

The ladies were still laughing over some of Georgia's less outrageous principles for properly training husbands when the gentlemen entered the salon. Juliana glanced at the mantel clock. Seldom had the men lingered so short a time.

"A pretty picture," Spencer remarked, strolling in and taking his customary chair next to the small sofa where Juliana and Miss Talbot sat talking. Violet was en-

sconced in the large wing-chair next to them, and Lord
Claypool lost no time in taking the matching chair beside her, settling his heavy bulk with a satisfied sigh.
Johnny glanced about with a look of comical dismay. He
had hoped for a chance to converse privately with Diana, but there was no place near her for him to sit, and
he'd enough of Basil's conversation.

"Miss Talbot, perhaps you would favour us with a
song on the harpsichord," he suggested blandly and offered her his arm. "I should be delighted to turn the
pages for you."

Diana looked hesitant, but Juliana, taking pity on her
brother-in-law, agreed that nothing would give them
more pleasure. Spencer hid his smile, bending forward to
fondle the ears of his spaniel, and Lord Claypool added
his opinion that nothing was more soothing to the diges-
tion than a bit of pleasant music. Violet nodded her en-
couragement, remarking that her daughter had a very
pretty voice.

Persuaded, Diana moved gracefully across the room
and seated herself at the harpsichord. It was a beautiful
instrument of inlaid mahogany, and she ran her slender
fingers over the keys, testing the tone, before looking
teasingly up at Johnny. "What do you wish, my lord?"

What he wished at that moment was not fit for a delicate young lady's ears, he thought, admiring the hollow
at the base of her throat that seemed to invite a man's
kiss. He had to restrain himself from reaching out to
touch her bare shoulder, and murmured something to the
effect that whatever she sang would be delightful.

Diana's hands faltered on the keys as she watched his
expressive eyes. Her breath caught and she was unaware
of the way her lips opened involuntarily.

"Diana, darling," her mother called, "sing that pretty ballad you learned in Bath. The one about the highway-man."

Recalled to her surroundings, Diana turned back to the keys, and felt the heat rising in her face. She sounded the first notes of the ballad and wished her mother had not requested that particular song. She sang softly, the tale of a dark-haired highwayman with laughing eyes who stole the hearts of the ladies while he lifted the gentle-men's purses. It fit too closely to Lord John, she thought, not daring to look at him again.

He, however, soon set her at ease with his light-hearted nonsense. He sang with enthusiasm, if not always on key, and a pleasant half hour passed before their hostess broke up the interlude.

"I must beg to be excused for a few moments," Juliana apologised. "It is my son's bedtime and though Spencer believes I am overly indulgent, I do like to say good-night before he sleeps."

"Oh, of course," Violet said at once. "I am completely in charity with your feelings. I was exactly the same with Diana. May I go up with you? I should dearly love to see your little boy."

The countess warmly agreed. She was never averse to showing off her son. Diana, too, was invited to view lit-tle Viscount Thornley, and the three ladies strolled up to the nursery.

Juliana tapped softly on the door and the nursemaid opened it at once, smiling gently. "He was just asking for you, my lady."

"Oh, he's beautiful," Diana cried, crossing the room to the foot of the tiny bed where John Louis sat amidst a pile of pillows, babbling happily at his company and reaching chubby arms up to his mother.

"Thank you, my dear. I rather think so, too. Spencer believes he looks much like Johnny did as a babe. I suppose it is the dark, curly hair."

Diana rather thought it was the crooked grin and lively blue eyes that put one in mind of his lordship.

"What a very good boy," Violet said in that tone some people invariably adopt when speaking to children. "May I hold him?"

"I should not advise it," Juliana said, laughing. "He loves to take the pins out of my hair and clutches at any piece of jewellery that catches his eye." She leaned forward and kissed the baby on his dark curls, deftly averting the chubby hand that grabbed at her necklace.

He laughed, clapping his hands and she ordered him sternly to go to sleep.

"Come along, ladies. Poppy will have him to sleep in a few moments. That, in truth, is when he is most appealing. He looks such an angel when he is sleeping."

Diana, who had paid scant attention to the nursery-maid, caught the unusual name and looked closer at the girl. It *was* the same girl, she thought, paling slightly, as she recognised the slender blond child she'd seen in Lord John's arms in Dover. She bit her lip and followed Lady Granville back into the hall.

"Have you...have you had your nurserymaid long?" Diana enquired as they passed through the long gallery.

"Why, no," Juliana said. "Only a week or so, though you would not think it to see her with John Louis. She is devoted to him and knows just how to manage him. I cannot tell you how delighted I am to have her, and I am enormously indebted to Johnny for that. He sent her to me from a place in Dover where the poor child was most unfairly given notice,'' she said, smiling. ''Another of his strays! But there, it has all happened for the best. Poppy is such a shy thing, I am certain she is much happier here than working at an inn.''

Diana nodded, unable to speak. She could not help looking at Lord John when they entered the salon with large, reproachful eyes. The audacity of the man. How dared he foist his cast-off *light skirt* onto his sweet and unsuspecting sister-in-law!

CHAPTER TEN

JOHNNY KNEW he needed to dismiss Diana Talbot from his mind and concentrate on the task at hand. Even without such distractions, it would be difficult enough to get Rousseau out of France. Besides, he told himself, no matter how he puzzled over her behaviour, there seemed to be no logical explanation for it. Diana had been cordial enough during dinner, and decidedly friendly while playing the harpsichord later. But when she'd returned from the nursery, there had been sufficient ice in her manner to freeze the Thames. He shook his head, determined to waste no more time on a lady whose emotions were more unpredictable than the weather.

And the weather was proving as contrary as ever. It had looked to be a pleasant morning when he and Jenkins had set out from London and his valet had remarked there'd been red skies the night before: a certain sign of good sailing weather and an easy Channel crossing. But five miles outside Dover, a storm had suddenly blown up and they arrived at the inn drenched from the pouring rain. Johnny had taken one glance at the churning sea and retreated to his room.

The retreat was of short duration. All too soon a dripping Jenkins reported a ship would be sailing in two hours. "It's not nearly as bad as it looks, my lord," he said, shaking the rain from his hat. "The sea's just a bit choppy, but there's no real wind."

Johnny looked out the dirty window, made even more opaque by the pelting rain, and nodded miserably. It was all of a piece: the new plan the duke had approved, Diana's strange behaviour and now the weather. He should have expected no less.

Jenkins poured his master a strong cup of coffee, surreptitiously adding a dollop of brandy, and then quietly left the room.

Johnny took a sip of the coffee, only half-aware of his actions. Despite his good intentions of putting her from his mind, thoughts of Diana continued to haunt him. He recalled the way her large brown eyes had reproached him—as though he had done something perfectly horrid. And it was not, as Spence later suggested, disapproval of his jaunt to France. She may have looked contemptuous when he'd casually mentioned that he was planning a short visit to Paris, but that was after she'd already made it quite clear that she regarded him as something lower than the lowest of species. It had been Spence who was indignant over his proposed trip.

"I should have thought you would have enough of jaunting about by now," he'd said, barely controlling his temper in front of guests.

"Oh, I have," Johnny replied, carefully smoothing the lace at his cuffs. "Indeed, the thought of another Channel crossing is quite abhorrent, but I fear a necessity. Juliana's cousin introduced me to his tailor, an extremely capable man. Really, Spence, you would benefit immensely by his skill. I was vastly impressed and ordered a half dozen coats from the fellow—which he writes are now ready—and I think you will deem it worth the trouble when you see how well they suit."

Spencer had stared at him as though he could not credit what he was hearing, and Juliana had hastily intervened, enquiring how long he would be abroad.

"No more than a fortnight, I should think, and possibly less if the weather proves co-operative."

Miss Talbot had made no comment beyond remarking she thought it was time they took their leave. It was after she and the others had departed that Spencer had given his temper free rein.

"It is little wonder the lady thinks you no more than a frippery fellow when it appears all you can think of is the cut of your coat. I vow it is enough to give any sensible person a disgust of you!"

"Spencer!" Juliana had hurriedly crossed to his side. "You know you do not mean such a thing." He stood stubbornly by the fireplace, his chin set in obstinate lines, and she turned appealingly to Johnny.

"Do not trouble yourself, Juliana. I am too accustomed to my brother's censures to take offence now. As for Miss Talbot, she appeared to have a disgust of me long before I mentioned this journey. Did something occur abovestairs to disturb her?"

"I noticed her manner became most strange," she replied, her eyes puzzled. "But we spoke only of John Louis and of Poppy. Indeed, I told her how you rescued the child and one would think that would endear you to her."

"One would think, but there is no accounting for the odd notions females take into their heads. Save for you," he added, and bent to kiss her brow. "Were there another like you, I would have been wed long since. Now I shall leave Spencer to your soothing ministrations and bid you a good night."

His brother had relented and walked with him to the door, stiffly enquiring if they would see him again before the journey. He recalled the way Spence had stood, obviously ill at ease, and the blue eyes, so like his own, sorely troubled. He had longed to confide the truth to Spence, but had, at the last, made a joke of it. "It's no use expecting me to live up to your standards, Spence— you set too high a measure and will only keep disappointing yourself! Really, I'm not such a bad fellow, you know."

"I know," he'd answered soberly. "And if you would only—well, never mind. Perhaps I do expect too much."

They had clasped hands and Johnny had turned to the door when Spence suddenly added, "Johnny? You do know there is no one I would rather have for a brother?"

"The feeling is mutual, old fellow," he'd replied, grinning to cover his own emotion.

They had parted on excellent terms, but Johnny took pains to avoid his brother for the next two days. He would see Spence when he returned and could tell him the truth. *If he returned.* The thought rose unbidden and Johnny stirred restlessly, but it was something that had to be faced. He was uneasy over this trip and had, for the first time, taken the precaution of leaving a sealed letter with Jenkins. He could trust his valet to deliver it to Spence if anything happened to him. And he could trust his brother to find a way to look after Diana.

Jenkins tapped softly on the door and stepped in. "It's time, my lord."

FOR NEARLY TEN DAYS after the dinner party, Diana Talbot was deeply troubled by recurring thoughts of Lord John. It annoyed her. That she had allowed herself, if only for the space of a few hours, to succumb to Lord

John's infamous charm was reprehensible enough. That he continued to frequently occupy her thoughts, in spite of her knowledge of his base character, was clear evidence of her own depravity. She made a conscious effort not to think of him, and was nearly successful, but she could not entirely banish him from the deep recesses of her mind.

She awoke slowly the following Tuesday, snuggling beneath the quilt and reluctant to give up her pleasant dreams. Her maid called her twice before she finally opened her eyes and struggled awake. It was several minutes before she recalled what had induced such a delightful feeling, and then her cheeks flushed warmly. *Madcap Johnny.* She'd dreamt of him again: imagined herself in his arms and rapturously returning his kisses!

Diana swung her legs out of bed, dismissing her maid with unusual curtness. She dressed rapidly, not caring in the least what she wore, and pulled the comb through her curls so roughly that her head ached. It was no more than she deserved. How *could* she allow herself to even think of Lord John when she was practically engaged to the Black Domino? She had allowed the Domino to kiss her, to embrace her warmly, on two different occasions. Any young woman with an ounce of morality would not behave so brazenly if her heart was already given. And it was, she insisted to herself. This...fascination with Lord John was a passing thing. She would not give him a second thought were Lord Brownlow in Town.

Her mirror image gazed back at her, unconvinced, and Diana fled the room. She hurried down the stairs but paused in the hall to compose herself. Her mother and grandmother were down before her, and she could hear the lively chatter of their voices and the yapping of the pugs in the breakfast parlour. Lifting her chin a fraction and forcing a smile to her lips, she pushed open the door and bade the ladies a cheerful good-morning. Carefully stepping over one of the pugs, she made her way round the table to her customary seat.

"Good morning, Diana," Lady Throckmorton said, eyeing her granddaughter critically as she handed her a cup of tea. "There are shadows under your eyes, my girl. Did you not sleep well?"

"Tolerably," she replied, sipping the tea and wishing her grandmother did not possess such sharp vision.

"I am not surprised," Violet said. "I hardly slept at all myself. This news about the Black Domino is most disturbing, though hardly unexpected. Basil said the man was pressing his luck, and after our last experience abroad, well, one could see how seriously the French were taking him. No doubt someone turned him in to collect the reward."

Diana's throat closed and her hand tightened about her cup. For a long moment she was incapable of speaking. She took a sip of tea, the hot liquid helping to ease the tightness in her chest and dryness of her mouth. "I—I did not hear the news. Have they caught the Domino, then?"

Violet's attention was on the copy of the *London Gazette* and she did not notice her daughter's sudden pallor. "Not yet. But it is believed he is fatally wounded. He was shot while trying to help a spy escape and they expect to apprehend him at any time. The French have issued a warning that any person caught aiding him will be arrested."

"It was a trap," Lady Throckmorton told her while buttering a bun and feeding it to the pugs. "I am astonished he was stupid enough to be caught in it. Any fool could see what they were doing."

"May I see the paper?" Diana asked, giving up all pretence of eating.

Violet passed her the sheet. "Basil mentioned it last night at Mrs. Drummond's—oh, you must have been dancing when we were all discussing it. Well, Sir Andrew Westfeld just arrived in Town straight from Calais, and he said you never saw such an uproar. Worse than when that Napoleon escaped." She stretched a hand across the table to pat Diana's. "I know how much you admired the gentleman, my dear, and I am sorry to tell you that it appears there is little hope of his escaping this time. Sir Andrew said every port is closely guarded and no matter how unlikely the prospect, every gentleman is being detained and examined to make certain he is not wounded. I fear this is the end of the Black Domino."

Diana tried to read the report in the paper but the words blurred before her eyes and she rose shakily, begging to be excused.

"Sit down and eat your breakfast, Diana," Lady Throckmorton ordered. "I will not have you dramatising this. After all, it is not as though you actually knew the man."

"But she did," Violet objected and as two startled pairs of eyes turned in her direction, added hastily, "In a manner of speaking. Diana has followed all his exploits and I am sure she knows more about the Black Domino than—oh, dear." She broke off suddenly, staring at the door.

"Good morning!" Emily trilled, walking heavily across the room. "Have you heard the news? Is it not prodigiously exciting?" she asked, waving her own copy of the *Gazette*.

"Come in, Emily, and do try to conduct yourself with a little more decorum," Lady Throckmorton said, and then motioned to Diana. "I find it a trifle cool this morning. Be so good as to bring me one of my shawls."

Diana gave her a tremulous smile and hurried from the room before Emily could see the tears standing in her eyes. At least her grandmother had provided her with a few moments' reprieve.

Emily, full of her news, noticed nothing amiss. "Mr. Bottomham is certain it will all come out now, and he believes the Domino to be a member of the aristocracy. Would it not be thrilling were it someone we actually know?"

"Hardly," her great-aunt said dryly. "Considering the man is not likely to survive, I should hate to think it might be someone with whom we are acquainted."

"Oh, well there is that, of course," she replied, momentarily daunted.

"I do not think we should be discussing it," Violet murmured. "Surely, it cannot be good for you to dwell on such unpleasantness in your condition?"

Emily did not consider the subject to be at all unpleasant. It was by far the most exciting news she'd heard in days, but mindful of her desire to appear all that was proper in front of her aunt, she reluctantly agreed and allowed Violet to turn the conversation.

When Diana rejoined them, the ladies were discussing Lord Salisbury's ball in honour of his daughter's engagement. It promised to be *the* ball of the Season, but unfortunately Emily had not received one of the coveted invitations and she consequently decried the lavishness and ostentatious expense of such an affair.

"It is quite ridiculous the extraordinary measures some people will take merely to attract attention. Why, do you know there is not a single blossom to be had in Town just now? Lady Salisbury has commandeered every available flower to embellish her ballroom. Poor Mr. Bottomham was most apologetic yesterday when he could not present me with roses, which you must know is his custom each week."

She paused, watching Diana's slender figure glide round the table and slip gracefully into her chair. Her eyes narrowed with envy and she continued spitefully, "Of course, I suppose it is understandable. Lady Salisbury must be fairly jubilant to get her daughter off her hands at last. Poor Claudia has had so many Seasons, I declare I have lost count. She made her first come-out with you, did she not, cousin?"

Diana looked up. She had heard Emily aimlessly chattering but had paid scant heed to her words. "I beg your pardon?"

"I was saying—oh, pray disregard it. It was nothing of import," her cousin replied, waving her plump fingers in dismissal, but noting with interest Diana's reddened eyes and pale complexion. "Is it merely my fancy, or are you feeling a trifle out of sorts, Diana? You look unusually pale this morning. I do hope you have not received any disappointing news?"

"No—no news of any sort," she replied with an effort to sound civil, and prayed Emily would not ask after the viscount.

They were interrupted by a footman bearing a large bouquet of roses. At Lady Throckmorton's nod, he entered and carried the flowers round the table to Diana. "These was just delivered, miss."

"Thank you, James," she said, her voice shaking slightly and her hand trembling as she removed the card.

"It appears you were wrong, Emily," Violet said with a slight smile. "Someone was able to procure a great number of roses."

Her face flaming with embarrassment, Emily helped herself to a cup of tea and muttered, "I should like to know how it was managed. Mr. Bottomham told me he visited several florists and there was not a single rose to be had. Who are they from, cousin?"

Diana did not answer. She sat staring dumbly at the card in her hand unable to believe the words scrawled on the card.

"Diana? Child, what is it? Who has sent such an extravagant bouquet?" Lady Throckmorton demanded, her loud voice disturbing the pugs at her feet. Dulcie roused herself sufficiently to sit up and growl low in her throat, which set the other two dogs yapping.

Emily carefully pushed her chair back and moved her legs to one side away from the creatures, but she was determined not to move from her seat until her cousin replied. There was something very strange about the way Diana was acting.

"It is from . . . Lord Brownlow," Diana said at last in a low voice, and passed the card to her grandmother. "He writes that if I will be at home tomorrow afternoon, he will give himself the pleasure of calling at four o'clock."

"Is that all?" Emily asked. "Well, I do not see what there is in that to put yourself in a taking. Goodness, for a moment I thought you would surely faint. Unless—you do not suppose he means to make an offer?"

The last was suggested with less than enthusiasm and Lady Throckmorton frowned at her niece. "I should not be at all surprised, Emily, or displeased."

"No, of course not, Aunt Henrietta . . . only my cousin does not appear to be precisely elated by the notion."

"It is just that I am surprised," Diana murmured. "I believed Lord Brownlow to be out of Town at present.

Would you excuse me, please? I must put these in some water.''

"Well!" Emily said when Diana had disappeared. "I still say she is behaving most peculiarly, and not at all like a young lady about to receive a respectable offer."

Violet Talbot laid aside her napkin and rose. "I will just have a word with her. Excuse me, please." She left the table before her mother could object and hurried after Diana. She found her in the small salon, standing before the sideboard, one rose in her hand and the rest of the enormous bouquet still lying in the sheath of tissue paper beside a tall vase.

"Diana? What is wrong, my dear?"

"Oh, it's you, Mama. Is Emily still here?"

Her mother nodded. "She's with your grandmother in the breakfast parlour. Diana, are you having doubts about Lord Brownlow?"

"Not doubts but . . . well, sometimes I believe I do not really know him at all," she confided, putting the single rose in the vase. "He does not always behave as I would expect."

"Men seldom do," Violet said, putting an arm about her daughter. "Darling, I have not had an opportunity to tell you yet, but Basil offered for me last night."

"Mama!"

"Hush. I've not told your grandmother, either, and must do so this morning. But, Diana, you do see this means you need not marry anyone? Not unless it is what you wish. Basil has already said he would be delighted to have you make your home with us."

"It is wonderful news, Mama, and I could not be happier for you," Diana said, hugging her, tears in her eyes.

Violet drew back and gently wiped the delicate drops from her daughter's cheek. "I wanted you to know so you would not worry over Lord Brownlow's call tomorrow. Now I shall go and break the news to Mother and to Emily—which I assure you is something I shall enjoy excessively."

Diana smiled and watched her go. Her mother was beginning to regain something of the spirit she'd had when she was younger. Her marriage would answer very well, she thought, and looked again at the roses before her. She should have been cast in raptures at receiving the bouquet. It must mean that somehow Lord Brownlow had escaped the French and was back safely, and for that she could only be devoutly thankful. *But why had he sent two dozen red roses instead of the one black rose he'd promised?*

JUST SOUTH OF St. Omer in the little town of Aire, Johnny awoke in the early hours of the morning and swore fluently. A dozen rats scurried for shelter as he stamped his feet and cursed them. He used his hat to beat at the side of the cot where Rousseau lay sleeping, and had the dubious satisfaction of sending two more of the rodents into hiding. The hut, little more than a shed, had been uninhabited for years except for the rats and spiders. It was fit for little else and hardly sufficient shelter for the pair of them, but for the moment it offered safety.

Jean-Baptiste opened his eyes and watched the younger man pace restlessly about the cramped hut. The Frenchman had expected an older, more experienced agent, but the past few days with the Domino had erased any doubts he'd harboured about the man's capabilities. If anyone could get them out of France in one piece, it was this man. But even with the young Englishman's uncanny skills, their chances at survival were slim.

Rousseau felt a deep remorse for leading the Domino into a trap, though he'd had little choice. He was not as ill as he'd led his guards to believe, but the fever that plagued him had hampered their efforts and slowed them down. There was no doubt it was the cause for the Domino taking a bullet in the shoulder. He had tried to apologise to the Englishman, but the man had shrugged it off as nothing.

It was more than a flesh wound, Rousseau knew that much, and it had bled profusely. Even now, he could see the dark blood staining the white bandage the Domino had fashioned from his cravat. It should be properly tended to and the bandage changed, he thought, or the young man could lose his arm. He'd warned him, but the Domino had stubbornly refused to seek help. "Better to lose my arm than our lives," he'd said. And Rousseau knew it to be the truth. The reward was too tempting.

Johnny noticed he was awake and crossed swiftly to his side, kneeling by the cot. His voice was a low whisper, but he smiled at the older man. "Good morning, *monsieur*. You see, we have survived another day in spite of your grim prophesies."

"And now?" Rousseau asked, his voice weak with effort.

"It depends on you," Johnny said. "If we can reach St. Omer today, I think there may be hope for us. Do you think you can walk so far?"

Rousseau nodded. It would be difficult, but if they went slowly—and if they could find something to eat . . .

"Then let us leave this grand hotel at once," Johnny said, his devilish grin once more in place. "I promise you shall find accommodations in England much more to your liking."

"Only let us get there," Rousseau murmured.

"We will," Johnny rashly promised and turned away before Rousseau could see the sudden pain in his eyes. His arm felt as though it were on fire. He tried to dull the agony by concentrating on other things. During the night he'd dreamed of Diana; dreamed of the way he'd held her in his arms at the masquerade and the way she'd responded so passionately to his kisses. Now, in the harsh grey light of the morning, all he could envisage was the reproachful look in her eyes the last night they'd met. He prayed he'd have another chance to convince her that they belonged together and with his prayers came a surge of determination. He would get back to England or die trying.

Rousseau was struggling up, his body shaken by a racking cough. Johnny left him to prepare for the gruelling trek to St. Omer and stepped outside for a look round. The hut was situated in the middle of a large wooded area dominated by tall pines, probably an abandoned game warden's hut, though there had been no sign of any game, much to his regret. Just the thought of a wild pheasant was enough to set his stomach growling.

Johnny spun about at a noise behind him, but it was only the Frenchman emerging from the hut. He used the stout branch Johnny had cut as a cane and limped forward.

"I am ready."

Johnny doubted it. A stiff wind would blow the man over. His body was so thin that one could count the bones beneath the pale skin, and his dark eyes still held a feverish look. Rousseau needed nourishing food and rest, but he was not likely to get either. Not in France.

The unlikely pair set off, moving as quietly as possible through the woods, and using the sun to keep them heading north. At least they were not burdened by a lot of excess baggage, Johnny thought. All they had was the clothes they wore, if their pitiful rags could be called such. They had outwitted the French by hiding beneath a bridge in a stream, up to their necks in the brackish water. The ruse had worked and their clothes had dried, but they were in tatters and stank to the heavens. Johnny smiled ruefully, thinking of Jenkins. His valet would likely disown him, were he to see him now.

Rousseau stumbled and Johnny reached out a hand to steady him. "Rest here for a few minutes," he ordered softly and helped the Frenchman to settle beneath a tall ash tree. "I'll scout ahead and see if there's any sign of our friends."

They had halted at the bottom of a small hill. Johnny's keen hearing had caught the slight sound of horses beyond the rise, and he suspected the road to St. Omer lay just ahead. He climbed up stealthily, using the trees as a protective shield until he was near the top of the rise. Then he dropped down and crawled. It was slow going. His left arm was almost useless. He positioned himself with all his weight on the other and inched slowly forward until he could look down on the road.

It was well he'd taken the precaution. A small troop of French soldiers rode past, loudly berating an old couple in a lumbering wagon for blocking the road. They shouted rude jests that the old man ignored and there were hoots of derision as they passed on either side of the dilapidated cart.

Johnny watched them for several moments, but none of the soldiers so much as glanced towards the woods. He suspected they were off duty and making their way to town, interested in nothing more than a large pint of ale or bottle of wine. That would change quickly enough if they suspected the Black Domino was within reach.

He pushed backwards, edging slowly down the rise until it was safe enough to stand, and then hurried back to where he'd left Rousseau. The Frenchman barely lifted his head as he heard Johnny approaching, and looked near to exhaustion. Johnny crouched beside him.

"St. Omer is just over the hill. We have to cross the road here and then head west. If you can manage it, I think I can promise you food and shelter within an hour." Johnny stared into the dark eyes, willing the man to find the strength to continue on. He didn't like to think of the alternative.

"I have little choice," Rousseau whispered. He knew as well as Johnny that he could not be left alive. "Let us go."

Johnny helped him up, breathing a prayer of gratitude. "This way," he said softly. "We will keep to the trees as much as possible."

The worst ordeal was crossing the road. It was beyond Rousseau to move rapidly, and once over the hill they were clearly exposed. Johnny drew his pistol, though without any shot it was fairly useless. Still, it might frighten someone and it felt comforting to hold it in his hand.

They waited at the top of the rise until Johnny was certain he could not hear the approach of horses in either direction. "Now," he ordered and with his good arm half supporting, half dragging Rousseau, they stumbled down the hill and across the road. They still had a long field to cross before they reached the shelter of the far woods, but the grass was waist-high and would conceal them from anyone on the road.

Johnny allowed Rousseau to sink down in the meadow for a few moments to gain his breath. His own heart was racing, as well, but he couldn't be comfortable until they gained the relative safety of the woods. He urged Rousseau to his feet. "Think of a hot bath, good food and a soft bed," he whispered. "This will all be over soon."

Rousseau nodded. He had no strength left to speak and he leaned more and more on the Englishman. It seemed much longer than an hour that he trudged helplessly beside the Domino. Every time he faltered, the man urged him on with the promise that it was only a few more steps. He was near the end of his endurance and half fell to the ground when the Domino finally motioned for them to halt.

Johnny barely noticed. He stood at the edge of the wood surrounding the rear of Louis Chevron's house and prayed he'd guessed right about the man's character. His life was in Chevron's hands. There was some movement near the barn and he stepped quickly back into the shadows of the pines.

"What…what now?" Rousseau asked, watching him warily.

"This house belongs to a cousin by marriage. I think we can trust him, but I must figure a way to get a message to him without alerting the servants. Wait—is it Sunday?"

Rousseau sighed. "I've no idea. Does it matter?"

Johnny did not answer. He stared intently at the activity in the stable yard. He knew Louis allowed most of the servants a half day off on Sundays. If the house was deserted, he'd have a chance of entering without being observed.

"Will you wait here? I'm going to try to get into the house. If I am successful, I'll come back with my cousin to help you."

"And if you are not?"

Johnny shrugged. "Pray that I am."

Rousseau knew he'd been given a reprieve and that the Englishman was taking a tremendous risk. The Domino had to be under orders not to leave him alive. He watched him for as long as he could, saw him slipping in and out of the shadows and finally disappear. Rousseau's head fell forward and he slipped unconscious to the ground.

Johnny crept round the garden, knowing the door to the terrace was his best chance. It always stood open during the day, or at least it had when he'd visited Louis. He stood for a few moments at the edge of the terrace, partially concealed behind a hedge, and straining his ears to pick up any sounds from the salon. There was nothing. The quiet preyed uneasily on his nerves.

One step forward to the terrace and he would be clearly exposed to anyone waiting inside. He hesitated and then moved out of concealment, lifting his head and strolling through the door as though he were a welcome guest. Louis Chevron was waiting for him.

Johnny saw him at once, sitting comfortably in a padded armchair, a brandy decanter and glass on the small table beside him. Louis glanced up and casually laid aside his book. He blew a circle of smoke in the air over his head.

"I thought you might pay me a visit, my lord," Louis said and stood.

Johnny remained still, his blue eyes watchful.

Louis smiled suddenly and opened his arms. "Come in, cousin. You are among family now and there is nothing to fear. I hoped, if my suspicions were correct, that you would turn to me if you needed help."

"You knew?" Johnny asked, raising a brow and accepting the embrace of the slender Frenchman.

"Not with any certainty, but yes, I suspected. But what is this?" he asked, looking at the tattered bandage on Johnny's arm. "The reports were true, then—you were wounded? *Mon Dieu!* We must attend to that at once."

"Not yet. There is something else that must be done," Johnny said reluctantly. "I have Rousseau with me. He is in the woods near the gate."

"You have succeeded, then! I never would have believed it possible, not even for the Black Domino."

"It very nearly was not," he answered with a tired sigh. "And Rousseau is not well. Will you help me, Louis?"

"Need you ask? We, who share a nephew named for the pair of us?"

"It is terrible risk you take. I would not ask it of you were there any other choice."

Louis shrugged. "You forget my mother was English. My loyalties are divided, but in this case family must outweigh all other considerations. You are safe with me, cousin."

Johnny cast a look of longing at the brandy, but knew it must wait until they had Rousseau safely in the house. He led the way, quietly answering Louis's questions and giving him the details of the torturous route they had taken from Mantes. Rousseau was unconscious when they found him, and it took nearly half an hour before they could revive him sufficiently to move him. Johnny and Louis supported him between them and half carried him back to the house.

Louis apologised when he led the way up to the attic to the old servants' quarters. They were no longer used, and it was the one place in the house where he could trust the servants not to venture.

"You understand, Johnny? The reward on your head is a fortune to these people. I do not believe they would betray me, but the risk is too great to take."

Johnny looked at the two narrow beds set up in the sparsely furnished room. The finest chamber in his brother's house had never looked so inviting, and he waved aside Chevron's apologies. "This is more than I have any right to expect. Thank you, Louis."

Johnny slept for six straight hours. When he awoke he found his arm had been freshly bandaged, and a tray stood on a small table near the bed. It contained a pitcher of cool spring water, clean glasses, a loaf of bread, large chunks of cheese and freshly sliced ham. "Bless you, Louis," he murmured.

Rousseau stirred an hour or so later. He was slightly feverish, but looked a great deal better for the rest. Johnny helped him to sit up and indicated the tray. "Eat sparingly," he warned as the Frenchman reached greedily for the bread.

They did not see Louis for several hours. He waited until the servants had settled in for the night and then silently climbed the stairs and tapped lightly on the door. Johnny was waiting for him. He had a plan, and if Louis were willing to assist them, they could be in England the next evening.

"But so soon?" Louis protested. "You are not rested yet and Monsieur Rousseau is far from well. I thought two or three days—"

"It is kind of you," Johnny interrupted. "But every hour we are here puts you deeper in danger. And there is another reason I must return tomorrow. On Tuesday, my man will deliver a letter to my brother and Juliana."

"I see," Louis said, sinking down on the bed beside him. "Well, then. What is to be done?"

Johnny blessed Juliana for having such a cousin and hurriedly outlined his plan. Louis considered it and then with a broad smile, nodded. "Yes, I think it can be done, but you will need help." He stood up and with shining eyes announced, "I shall come with you. In the morning I will make all the arrangements."

Johnny stared at him. "I cannot allow it. You have done too much for us as it is. If we are caught—"

"Caught? The Black Domino? Bah, I do not think it. Besides, I go to visit my little nephew, John Louis, eh? It will be a nice surprise for Juliana, no?"

CHAPTER ELEVEN

THEY HAD DECIDED on Calais. It was the closest port to St. Omer and according to Louis, every port was so heavily patrolled that it hardly made any difference which they chose. "Either our plan will work or it will not," he said with a fatalistic shrug.

Johnny had agreed. It had been absurdly easy to do so in the narrow confines of the attic room, but as they neared the Hotel Angleterre he was not so certain the choice was a wise one. French soldiers were everywhere. The next hour would prove crucial.

There was one point in their favour. Louis Chevron had had the good sense to make their sailing arrangements in advance. He'd ridden to Calais as soon as it was light and booked passage on a cutter leaving that afternoon, and then procured the baggage and apparel they needed for the journey. The three of them would arrive just two hours before departure. It was barely sufficient time to pass through customs.

But even an hour or two under the relentless scrutiny of the soldiers could prove fatal, Johnny thought, as he stepped down from the carriage in the courtyard and turned to help Jean-Baptiste. The Frenchman, swathed in yards of black cambric, was playing the part of an elderly and very ill widow. The ugly red splotches Louis had painted on his face looked horridly real beneath the black netting of the huge hat Louis had provided him.

Rousseau moved shakily, hunched over a cane, which helped to disguise his height.

Johnny, dressed in black silk, bent solicitously over him, while silently cursing the corset Louis had insisted on lacing him into. The tight stays pinched him unmercifully every time he moved.

"*Pardon, mademoiselle,*" a guttural French voice said behind him.

Johnny looked round without straightening.

"Are you in need of assistance?" the soldier asked with a slight bow.

"*Merci,*" he murmured, pitching his voice as high as possible and fluttering a gloved hand. "*Ma grandmère* is very ill, but I should not like to endanger you." He shrugged. "The doctor said she is not contagious, but…" He allowed the words to trail off and stepped slightly away so the soldier could see Rousseau's splotchy face.

The soldier backed away and, muttering about his duty, quickly retreated. Louis, dressed demurely as a serving maid, hid a triumphant smile and helped Johnny get Rousseau into the Custom House. He found chairs for the unlikely pair, explaining to everyone possible that the old woman was deathly ill. As Louis predicted, they were given a wide berth, and he felt safe in leaving them to bring in their baggage.

Once the two trunks and valise were safely in, he stood in line until he had the attention of a customs officer. Nodding deferentially, he begged the gentleman to come to Madame Chevron's chair. "She is most ill, sir, and cannot stand for long."

The officer looked across the room to where Louis pointed. "Why is she travelling, then?" he demanded.

"Her sister died in England, sir. We go for the funeral, though I fear it may be her own, as well. *Ma-*

dame's health is not at all good and the red marks on her face worry me. The doctor said it is nothing, but me—I do not think it. I recall an old man who had such marks and he died—"

"Never mind," the officer interrupted. "Bring the baggage here and I will inspect it. No need to disturb the old woman."

Louis bobbed his head and thanked him profusely while backing away. He turned as soon as he was able and breathed a prayer of thanks. He could feel a trickle of sweat seeping beneath the blond wig and delicately dabbed at his head with a handkerchief while he crossed the room.

Two soldiers had entered and were standing near Johnny. Rousseau bent his head and succumbed to a fit of coughing which shook his body. The retching sound was enough to make the soldiers move away and Louis grinned at the pair as he approached. "Well done, my friend. That was most believable."

"He wasn't acting," Johnny whispered. "Try to hurry them along, Louis."

Chevron nodded and laboriously dragged the trunks across the room. Johnny was tempted to help, but Louis waved him back. "You are too tall, cousin. It is better you remain seated."

He was right, of course, but it was nerve-racking merely to sit there while French soldiers paraded in and out of the building. He had an uneasy notion of what a guillotine victim must feel, waiting for the blade to fall. Then Louis was back.

"I paid a boy to bring the baggage and we can board the ship now. There is much talk here about the Dom- ino. Most of the soldiers seem to believe he is dead, so perhaps that will help. They are not as observant as they should be."

"I hope you are right," Johnny said. He assisted Rousseau to rise, and stooped over as much as possible under the guise of helping the old woman to walk. Louis minced along a few paces ahead of them. He repeatedly announced the old woman was ill, and begged the people to clear a way. Johnny heard his sudden gasp and halted even as Louis turned to face him.

"It is Lieutenant Jennot," he whispered. "There by the door."

Johnny looked up. The lieutenant was not looking in their direction, but they would have to pass directly in front of him.

"Perhaps we should wait?" Louis suggested hesitantly.

"What is it?" Rousseau demanded, his breathing laboured.

"The lieutenant guarding the door knows me—knows me well," Johnny said and bent his head as Jennot looked in his direction. "We must continue. It would look strange if we halted now. Are you both game?"

The others nodded and Louis again walked ahead. He thought for a brief moment the lieutenant would allow them to pass without question. But he suddenly held out an arm, barring the way.

"Do you require assistance, *mademoiselle?*" Jennot asked, looking directly at Johnny. "Is the old woman ill?"

Louis answered him, his voice pitched high and simpering. "*Merci,* but we would not trouble you."

"I was not addressing you," Jennot answered curtly. "Where are you going, *mademoiselle?*"

"To England," Johnny answered and shifted Rousseau's weight so his right arm was free. He reached under his skirts and felt the reassuring weight of his pistol.

There was silence and he looked up into Jennot's eyes. He saw the flicker of recognition and braced himself. The lieutenant's hand moved to rest on his sword hilt, but he hesitated and Johnny saw the indecision in his eyes.

"Are you planning to return to France?" Jennot asked suddenly, his voice cold and hard and his dark eyes full of anger.

"No...I pledge my word this is my last visit," Johnny said slowly, praying he was correctly understanding the lieutenant.

Jennot nodded abruptly and turned away. They heard him speak loudly to the officer beside him, "I think we waste our time here. The Black Domino is dead."

DIANA WAITED impatiently for the viscount to appear. She had little notion what to expect. Would he be limping from a wound in his leg, or perhaps have his arm in a sling? Or were the rumours that the Black Domino had been badly wounded just rumours?

"You would do well to take up knitting," Lady Throckmorton advised, watching her granddaughter nervously tap her foot. "I declare you are as restless as a tom-cat on the prowl."

"Mother!" Violet protested.

"Plain speaking never hurt anyone," the old lady declared. "What has you in such a fret, Diana? It is not as though you never received an offer before. Heaven knows, you have turned down more gentlemen than I can recollect."

"Perhaps it is because she means to accept this one," Violet suggested, with a tender look for her daughter.

"Hmmph. I wish I might live to see it. You've spoiled her, Violet. You and Claypool, telling her she may live with you. A girl needs to be married, to have her own home. I hope you will not regret it—the pair of you— Where are you going, miss?"

Diana, who had arisen and crossed the room, paused by the door. "Up to my bedchamber. I am certain you will be more comfortable discussing my prospects without my presence. Have Simmonds call me when Lord Brownlow arrives."

"Impertinent chit."

Diana heard her grandmother but chose to ignore her and hurried up the stairs to the privacy of her room where she could give way to the attack of nerves besetting her. Brownlow would arrive in a very few moments and she had not yet decided how to answer him.

She sat down at the mahogany writing desk and opened the long drawer, carefully lifting out a black silk rose. A slight trace of perfume still clung to its petals and she closed her eyes, imagining again the night he'd given it to her. She could almost feel the strength of his arms embracing her and the intoxicating touch of his lips on hers.

A tap on the door interrupted her reverie, and she hastily replaced the rose before calling permission to enter.

"My lady said I should tell you Lord Brownlow is here, miss," Simmonds said sullenly, evidently resenting having to climb the stairs to find her.

"Thank you. I shall be down directly." She waited until the maid had closed the door, then crossed to stand in front of her looking-glass. She smoothed the skirt of the dark blue walking dress, brushed back a chestnut curl and took a deep breath. Perhaps her racing heart and indecisiveness were part of being in love. Perhaps merely seeing the viscount again would resolve her doubts.

When she entered the salon a few moments later, there was no outward sign of her agitation. She extended a hand to Lord Brownlow and presented him with a warm smile. Only her eyes contained a shadow of doubt as she searched for some sign of a wound. But the viscount looked in remarkably good health.

He held her hand for longer than was considered proper but the blood did not rush to her head. There was none of the delicious tingling she'd felt when he'd been masked, and no heady desire to cast herself into his arms. She withdrew her hand and managed to thank him with creditable composure for the lovely roses he had sent.

"Indeed, it was my pleasure, Miss Talbot."

"And so many, my lord," she said, arching her brows slightly. "One would have been quite sufficient."

"Oh, I am not such a paltry fellow as that," he laughed, not understanding her allusion to the single promised rose. "Come, will you be seated. There is something of a particular nature I wish to say to you."

Diana hesitated. "I had thought to find you with my mother and grandmother."

"Lady Throckmorton granted me permission to see you alone. You need not fear we will be interrupted, my dear."

Diana allowed him to lead her to the sofa and, once seated, glanced up at him. Lord Brownlow was undeniably handsome. His blond hair was brushed into the latest style and his tan coat was superbly tailored to his broad shoulders and marched well with his dark waistcoat and buff pantaloons. Why, then, did she have the feeling something was drastically wrong?

She saw him remove a small box from his waistcoat. She recognised it as coming from Rundle & Bridge Jewellers, and spoke hurriedly to postpone the moment when she must make a decision. "I am surprised, my lord, to find you looking so well. I confess, knowing what business took you out of Town, that I was fearful I should find you wounded."

"Wounded? Now, what put that notion in your head?" he asked, watching her closely. The business he'd lately been involved in was sufficient to land him in Newgate were he caught, but he doubted Diana could possibly know anything of it, else she would not have received him.

"I have heard the rumours, my lord. Surely, there is no longer any need of pretence with me?"

"No, of course not," he replied uneasily. "But I do not quite understand. What is it you wish to know?"

She rose quickly, eluding his hand and moving towards the window. She was certain now that she had been mistaken, terribly mistaken. She turned to face him, unable to think clearly. "I wondered when you sent all the roses . . . there should have been a black rose . . ."

"My dear Diana, once we are wed you may have all the roses you wish, red, yellow or black," he promised persuasively, while wondering if the girl were demented.

"You truly do not understand," she said slowly. "But at the masquerade—"

"Is that what this is about?" he interrupted. "I explained to you, my dear, that it was not certain I would be able to attend. I did try, of course, but you must understand that business comes before pleasure. There will be other masquerades," he added, taking a step towards her.

"You were not in France, after all," she said suddenly, the words an accusation.

"Not since I met you in Dover, but what has that to say to anything? Come, Diana, you are behaving most strangely. Sit down, my dear, and allow us to discuss this reasonably."

She stepped backwards, again avoiding his outstretched hand and shaking her head. "I am sorry, my lord, but there is nothing to discuss. I believe it would be best if you took your leave."

He checked an angry retort and turned, bending his head so she could not see the fury blazing in his eyes. Everything was in order. As soon as the engagement was announced, his financial problems would be over. He could not afford to allow her to withdraw now.

Diana mistook his bowed head for sorrow and felt a measure of remorse. She laid a hand upon his sleeve and spoke softly. "I am indeed, sorry, my lord. I find I was...mistaken in my feelings. If I have unwittingly caused you pain, I regret it most sincerely and must beg your forgiveness."

The viscount turned away from her, thinking rapidly. He could not allow Miss Talbot to elude him. Everything depended on her. He still toyed with the box in his hand and he opened it, removing the ring and holding it up to the light. "I had hoped for the honour of putting this on your hand today and the joy of announcing our engagement. I am...at a loss to know what to say. I suppose it was arrogant of me to presume—"

"Oh, no," she cried, moved by his distress. "Not at all. I know I gave you reason to suppose I should welcome an offer from you. It was foolish of me. I am truly sorry, my lord."

He sighed and restored the ring to its box. "Thank you, my dear. I am sure I shall recover, given time. Might I ask one last favour of you, Miss Talbot?"

"Certainly, my lord. If there is anything I can do, you have only to ask," she promised rashly.

"I have engaged a box for us at Vauxhall Gardens this evening—a celebration of sorts, and my aunt, Lady Stapleton, has agreed to act as hostess. Will you come? Please? It is just a small party of friends—people whom I wished to introduce you to—and they will all be expecting to meet you this evening. It will save me a great deal of embarrassment if you would consent to be my guest. I know it is a lot to ask, but I find I cannot face them just yet with the truth."

She could not refuse. It was, after all, very little that he asked, and she had placed him in an embarrassing position with his friends. She smiled. "I should be pleased to come, my lord."

"Wonderful, my dear. I shall call for you at seven. Now, if you will excuse me, I shall slip out before I encounter your grandmother."

Diana wished she could leave with him. Her grandmother was not going to be pleased with the news that she had rejected yet another suitor. Perhaps she could tell her that the viscount had not proposed. That much was true; she hadn't given him the opportunity. She sighed, wishing she were more certain of her feelings. All she could think of was the Black Domino. She had been mistaken in believing him to be the viscount, but if not Lord Brownlow, who then, had given her the black rose? And was he still in France? Perhaps fatally wounded as the rumours implied? So engrossed was she in her thoughts that she nearly collided with Simmonds outside the door of the salon and hastily begged pardon.

Diana successfully avoided telling her grandmother and mother of the viscount's offer and mentioned only the evening party planned for Vauxhall. Violet misliked the notion. Both she and her mother were engaged for the evening and neither would be able to accompany Diana. But Lady Throckmorton dismissed her objections, declaring she saw nothing amiss with the scheme. Lady Stapleton would be at Vauxhall to ensure the young people kept to the line, and after all, she pointed out, the couple were nearly engaged. When Diana added her pleas, Violet reluctantly gave her consent, with the result that the ladies were able to greet Lord Brownlow with comfortable complacency later that evening.

Diana thought the viscount was in a most peculiar mood. She set it down to his disappointment and chattered about the various routs and rumours that were the latest on-dit. When she continued to meet with silence, she grew restive and raised the shade on her side of the carriage. Brownlow abruptly reached across to stay her hand, but it was too late. She'd seen the direction they were taking and turned to him with a puzzled frown.

"This is not the way to the Gardens. Where are you taking me, sir?"

"For a very long drive, Miss Talbot, or perhaps I should say, Diana, since we will shortly be on the most intimate of terms."

She stared at him, aghast, as his meaning dawned. "I demand you let me out of this carriage at once."

"I am sorry, my dear, but that is quite impossible. A note will be delivered to your grandmother late this evening, informing her that we have decided to fly to Gretna Green. I fancy Lady Throckmorton will be a bit miffed at an elopement, but in the end quite pleased that you have finally agreed to become my wife. She rather favours my suit, you know."

"I will never marry you," she swore, reaching for the door handle.

A hand like a band of steel captured her fingers and twisted them cruelly. "I warn you, Diana, I will not suffer any foolishness. I should hate to hurt you, my dear, but do not doubt I shall if you do not behave. And if you are thinking of screaming for the coachman, I must tell you he is under orders not to halt for any reason until we have reached Kettering. We stop there only to change horses."

"You cannot force me to marry you," she said furiously, rubbing her reddened wrist.

"Oh, I rather think I can. After spending an entire night in my company, you will have little choice, my dear."

IT WAS LATER that evening, when the sun was just setting across Regent's Park, that Johnny stepped down from the hired carriage in front of his rooms in Charing Cross. He paid the driver with the last of the pound notes he'd borrowed from Louis, and prayed he would find Jenkins back in Town. It was well he arrived at that odd hour when the ton had returned from their afternoon excursions but were not yet venturing forth for the evening. His appearance in a pair of ill-fitting trousers and disreputable-looking coat would have given rise to much comment.

Johnny rushed up the stairs and breathed a sigh of relief as Jenkins flung open the door.

"My lord! Praise the saints!" he cried, crossing himself. "I had near given you up for lost."

"Never count me out, Jenkins. How many times have I told you that?" he asked with an impudent grin as he entered and shrugged off the coat. "Burn this, will you?"

"Yes, my lord," his valet answered, handling the garment gingerly. "The trousers, too, sir?"

"By all means! I would have given a month's pay to have you with me in Dover this morning," he said, striding to the bedchamber and disrobing at once.

Jenkins followed faithfully, but now all his attention was on his lordship's appearance. His eyes noted at once the neat bandage round his arm, and despite Johnny's jubilant tone, there was a tired, weary look in his eyes. "So the reports you were wounded were true. I heard it at Dieppe and came home as you instructed, sir. Is it much painful?"

"What, this?" he asked, looking down at his arm. "Hardly a twinge. I had it looked at this morning, so don't be fretting over it. What I need now is a hot bath, a shave and some clean clothes."

"You'll never be going out this evening, sir?"

"I am. After you draw a bath, find Finley and tell him I shall have need of him. I must see the duke first, and then Miss Talbot." He halted, seeing his valet's face suddenly pale.

"What is it? Oh, good God! Tell me you did not deliver that letter to my brother yet!"

"No, my lord. Today is the fourteenth day. Had you not returned this evening, I would have on the morrow, but—"

"Then what is causing the Friday-face? Out with it, man."

"I am sure it is nothing, sir. Only... well, rumour has it that Miss Talbot received an offer from Lord Brownlow today."

"Did she, now? And does rumour have it what answer she returned?" he asked, a devilish light in his eyes.

"No, my lord, but Mrs. Simmonds, who is Lady Throckmorton's personal maid, told the butcher's wife that Miss Talbot is driving to Vauxhall Gardens with his lordship this evening. One would think, had she refused the gentleman, that she would not then accompany him to the pleasure gardens."

Johnny tossed his trousers to his valet and laughed. "You really should not listen to gossip, Jenkins. Now, how long do you intend to keep me waiting for my bath?"

Jenkins left the room a few moments later, muttering that his lordship was in a rare taking and it boded ill for someone. But even he had to admit his lordship did him proud when he stepped out the door a scarce two hours later. He wore a dark blue tailcoat, an elegant creation that, while it did not fit as tightly as a second skin, had the advantage of sliding easily over the bandage on his arm. The buff pantaloons, on the other hand, fit snugly against his thighs before disappearing into the high black boots. A distinctive blue-striped waistcoat, crisp linen shirt and expertly tied cravat proclaimed him a gentleman of discerning style.

He pulled on his gloves, disdained a cape, for the evening was warm, and hooked an ebony cane over his arm, before instructing Finley to drive to the Cardiff residence. They arrived in Belgrave Square as the clock was chiming seven. Thurgood informed him the duke was just sitting down to dinner. He reluctantly agreed, however, to convey a message to the duke, and Johnny had the satisfaction of seeing His Grace appear in the hall almost at once.

They were closeted in the library for close to an hour while Johnny described all that had transpired. He assured the duke again that Rousseau was safe at his brother's house and would be with him on the morrow, that Louis Chevron could be trusted to bring him safely to the house, and that the French believed the Black Domino to have died of his wounds. Despite his best efforts to keep the interview brief and his promises to answer all questions at length the following day, it was a few moments past eight before he could leave.

He ordered Finley to put the horses to a gallop and they arrived in Manchester Square in record time. He found the house in chaos. The butler answered his knock but it was Simmonds, standing just behind him, who told him flatly that Miss Talbot was out. "And we've no idea of when she may return," she added.

"Then I wish a word with Lady Throckmorton," Johnny persisted, blocking the door with his shoulder.

"Her ladyship is too distraught to see anyone," she began but broke off as a loud sobbing wail erupted from the drawing-room.

Johnny stepped past the butler and strode down the hall, following the sound of hysterical sobbing. He ignored Simmonds, half running to keep up with him and clutching at his coat, and stepped into the room where Lady Throckmorton was vainly trying to comfort her daughter.

Violet Talbot was sitting in one of the armchairs, clutching a tattered note in her hand, and sobbing incoherently. Her mother stepped in front of her and demanded furiously, "What is the meaning of this intrusion, sir? Simmonds, I told you to deny us."

"She tried," Johnny said, "but I think you may have need of me. Is Diana in trouble?"

Lady Throckmorton hesitated, wondering if it were yet possible to save her granddaughter from her own foolishness. "She may be, but I fail to see what concern it is of yours, my lord."

"I intend to marry her," Johnny answered bluntly. "And we are wasting time. What has happened?"

Lady Throckmorton observed him closely and then nodded. Leaning over, she extracted the note from her daughter's hands. "Read this, sir. It is from Lord Brownlow."

Johnny scanned the carelessly scrawled lines. "She is eloping with Brownlow? I do not believe it."

"Nor do I. Diana knows, if she wished to wed the viscount, she had my blessing. There was no need for an elopement...but she went with him willingly enough this evening. A footman gave Simmonds the note a few moments after she left."

He stepped round her and knelt beside Mrs. Talbot's chair, taking her trembling hands in his own. "Did Diana confide in you, ma'am? Do you believe she wished to wed Brownlow?"

Violet looked up tearfully and shook her head. "I was certain she would not . . . she was confused, and now—" She broke off, covering her face with her hands, sobs shaking her shoulders.

Johnny rose, trying to think what was best to do and caught sight of Simmonds, still hovering near the door. "What do you know of this?" he suddenly demanded.

"I? Why, nothing, my lord. Miss Talbot has always been a wilful girl, very headstrong. I am not surprised that she—"

"You are Simmonds, aren't you?" he interrupted. "You told some butcher or other that Brownlow offered for Diana today. Was that true?"

She nodded, darting a miserable glance at her mistress. "I—I was outside the salon and overheard them."

"You mean you had your ear pressed to the door," Lady Throckmorton said furiously. "Well, then? What was her answer? I'll have the truth, Simmonds, or you shall find yourself out on the street."

"She refused him," the maid whispered uneasily. "She said she'd mistaken her feelings."

"Why didn't you tell me this earlier?" the old lady demanded.

"I was only trying to help you, my lady," she said tearfully. "I know the girl was a drain on you and this way she'd be married off. I didn't think he would hurt her none."

"It hardly matters now," Johnny said. "But I think I am beginning to understand. It was after she refused him that his lordship proposed to visit Vauxhall, was it not?"

Simmonds nodded miserably. "He said he'd friends there, waiting to meet her and would be embarrassed if she refused to come. It was a favour, he said."

"So he lured her out with a tale of Vauxhall, intending all the while to elope," Johnny said and turned to Lady Throckmorton. "I am only surprised he left that note for you. Of course, you would have been concerned had she not returned at a reasonable hour...but why deliver it so soon?"

Simmonds sniffed. "He gave it to the footman when he was leaving. Harry said he was to give it to my lady in the morning, but tomorrow is his half day and he asked me to see she got it."

Johnny nodded and knelt once more beside Mrs. Talbot. "I am going after her, ma'am, and you must trust that I will bring her back to you this evening."

"Get me my coat, Simmonds," Lady Throckmorton demanded and to Lord John added, "I am going with you."

Johnny shook his head. "I shall be travelling fast, my lady. You would only be in the way."

"I do not intend to see you scotch one scandal by setting up another. You will have need of me, my lord, and I suggest we don't waste time standing here arguing."

CHAPTER TWELVE

"WHY AREN'T YOU driving yourself?" Lady Throck-morton demanded when they were settled in his carriage and heading out of London at a dangerous pace.

"Finley is an excellent coachman, my lady. You need not entertain any fear that he shall overturn us."

"When you get to be my age, you will learn there is very little worth fearing. I was merely questioning the need to employ a groom in a delicate business. It seems to me that the fewer people who know about this matter, the better for all concerned."

"He is completely discreet, my lady," Johnny an-swered curtly, cursing the arm that prevented him from driving himself.

"That's as may be, but hardly answers my question. It would not have anything to do with the stiff way you have been holding your left arm, would it, my lord?"

"You are most discerning. My arm is wounded—does that satisfy you?"

"Not entirely, since I had assumed as much. How did it occur?"

He gave her an exasperated look. "Does it matter?"

"Inasmuch as you have declared your intention of marrying my granddaughter, I believe it does."

"We must find her first," Johnny said grimly. "But if it will allay your anxieties, I will tell you that it was an honourable affair. Nothing that need trouble you."

"I shall be the one to decide that. I have a suspicion of what you've been up to, young man, and I warn you I will not allow Diana to wed you if that is the sort of life you intend to live, however honourable it may be."

His temper snapped. "Haven't you had enough of interfering in her life? It was your insistence that she marry which led to the evening."

He regretted his sharp words at once. Even in the dim light of the carriage, he could see her chins shake and her narrow lips start to quiver and knew he had hurt her deeply.

There was silence for several miles and then she suddenly spoke again. "I love Diana, you know. If I urged her to marry, it was only because I desired to see her happily settled."

"I know," he sighed. "I spoke out of turn. It is only that, had you not threatened to disinherit her—"

The old lady gave a bark of laughter. "There's nothing left to inherit, my lord. I have barely enough to live on myself. If you wed Diana, she will come to you penniless."

Johnny stared at her. "Then all the talk—"

"Was just that. I tried in every way I could think of to convince Diana to wed. My supposed fortune was the only means I had of making certain she would consider marriage."

"You might have tried telling her the truth," he said gently.

"Indeed," she replied with a trace of her old tartness. "It is a recommendation you should follow yourself, my lord. Have you been completely truthful with my granddaughter?"

Johnny had no answer and, after a futile glance out the window, leaned back against the seat. There was little hope of spotting Brownlow's carriage. No doubt it was a hired vehicle and in the dusk would be impossible to recognise. He concentrated on what he would say to Diana once he found her again.

The long nights he'd spent hiding in the woods with Rousseau had given him ample time to consider that young lady and her seemingly strange behaviour. He'd slowly come to the conclusion that she had no notion of his identity, despite her comments to the contrary. Of course, he'd suspected that all along, but had not considered the implications. Diana had been very certain she knew him; *ergo,* she must believe someone else to be the Black Domino. And given her stated admiration for Brownlow, the fact that he and the man were of the same weight and build and both possessed blue eyes, it was ridiculously easy to see where she had erred. Well, that was easily rectified, he thought, fingering the black silk rose nestled in his waistcoat pocket.

He was still a little troubled by the manner in which she'd rebuffed him at his brother's house, but Johnny thought he knew the reason for that, as well. He'd belatedly recalled little Poppy's grateful embrace at the inn just when Diana was passing down the hall. He smiled in the darkness of the carriage. It seemed the height of absurdity, but he was fairly sure she believed Poppy to be his cast-off mistress. *Foolish girl,* he thought. He would have to teach her to trust him.

The long hours stretched endlessly ahead. They stopped once at Dunstable and again at Northampton but were unable to learn anything of the viscount. Lady Throckmorton was growing discouraged, but Johnny remained confident that they would shortly be catching up to Brownlow, and he jumped down at the posting house in Kettering with an optimistic air.

Lady Throckmorton picked up the ebony cane he'd left in the carriage and descended, as well. She used it to support some of her weight and walked heavily round the carriage, stretching her stiff limbs.

Johnny found her there a few moments later and urged her back inside the carriage. "I believe they may be just ahead of us. One of the post boys said a gentleman changed horses here just twenty minutes past. He was travelling in a dark brougham and remained inside with the shades drawn, so the boys didn't get a look at him, but they were tipped heavily to make the change speedily."

"And Diana?" she asked fearlessly, climbing up the steps.

"One lad said he thought he heard a muffled shout, but couldn't be sure and the coachman kept him away from the carriage," he said, slamming the door and giving Finley the signal to start.

His face was set in grim lines and he sat stiffly, keeping an alert watch out the window as his groom sent the team flying. Lady Throckmorton held tightly to the carriage strap as it swayed precariously but never uttered a word of protest.

They had just passed through the mountains north of Kettering when Finley shouted. A brougham was just ahead. It proved no match for Johnny's team of bays and Finley passed the lumbering carriage with ease. He manoeuvred their own rig across the road, forcing the brougham to a halt. Johnny was out in an instant, his pistol drawn. The coachman threw up his hands and Johnny, keeping a wary eye on him, approached the carriage door.

The shade flew up and a white-haired gentleman nervously poked his purse out the window. "Don't shoot," he begged in a quavering voice. "Just take my purse and leave us be. We'll not fight you."

Johnny sighed and lowered the pistol. He offered an embarrassed apology and, much to the old gentleman's astonishment, beat a hasty retreat back to his own carriage.

"That was Sir Vincent Kingsly," Lady Throckmorton told him as he took his seat once more. "Do you think he recognised you?"

"No, he was too frightened to notice much."

"Perhaps you should have taken the purse," she mused. "It would have given him something to talk about beside his gout. I have been acquainted with him for years and it is the only conversation he has."

He glared at her, but whatever utterance he had in mind was bitten off as Finley shouted again. Another brougham was just ahead. Finley tried the same manoeuvre, but as he pulled alongside to pass, the driver of the brougham whipped his horses and the two carriages careened wildly down the hill.

"I pray your man remembers Diana may be inside that carriage," Lady Throckmorton murmured.

There was a bend in the road ahead and the driver of the brougham lost his nerve. He checked his horses on the curve, and Finley swept past and into the middle of the road before he began reining in his own team. It was several moments before he could bring the plunging bays to a halt.

The coachman saw him approaching with his pistol drawn and held up his hands. "I was only hired to drive the team," he yelled. "This is no business of mine."

Johnny ignored him, knowing Finley would keep an eye on the man, and positioned himself near the front of the carriage. "Brownlow! Let her go, Brownlow. The game is up."

The carriage door flew open and he saw a prettily shod foot kick at the door. He cursed fluently and edged forward. He could see Diana struggling to get free of the viscount but could not risk a shot for fear of hitting her. Brownlow held her in front of him, one arm wrapped beneath her neck.

Diana was no tame armful. She struggled to reach the door and when Brownlow moved his arm slightly to get a better grip, she swiftly bent her head and bit his hand.

He howled and let go of her long enough for her to scramble down the steps. Johnny motioned her out of the way and in a voice deadly with menace invited the viscount to step out.

"I am unarmed," Brownlow said, straightening the cuff on the sleeve where the little vixen had bitten him, and stepped down. "Would you shoot me in cold blood?"

Johnny tossed his own pistol to Finley and stripped off his coat. He ignored the protests of his groom. The sight of Diana struggling in Brownlow's arms had driven all thoughts from his mind save for an insane desire to strangle the man with his bare hands. He tossed his coat to Finley and stepped forward, landing a crashing right fist to the viscount's jaw.

Brownlow reeled from the impact but remained on his feet. "If it's a fight you want, my lord, I should be pleased to accommodate you. I've had sufficient of your meddling in my affairs and 'tis past time someone taught you a lesson." He peeled off his own jacket and with raised fists circled round Lord John.

Lady Throckmorton hobbled from the carriage and stood at the edge of the circle watching, leaning on Johnny's ebony cane.

"Grandmama!" Diana cried in amazement, hugging the older woman. "Oh, I am so thankful to see you. But how—?"

"Hush, child. We shall sort it all out later. At the moment, I am more concerned with your young man. That left arm of his is injured. Hardly a fair fight."

"Oh, no!" she cried, and whirled to watch the two men. They appeared evenly matched, but Johnny was clearly at a disadvantage. The wound he dismissed so lightly had sapped his strength and he was near exhausted from his journey. Only blind rage kept him on his feet.

Diana urged Finley to do something, but he shook his head, knowing better than to interfere, though he kept one of the pistols trained on the viscount.

Brownlow was in a rage. All his plans had dissolved and he was left facing financial ruin. He fought like a madman, raining blows on Johnny and barely feeling the punishing right fist that rocked his chin at every opportunity. He found an opening and landed a telling blow on Johnny's left arm. He sensed the other was weakening and his sharp eyes caught the signs of blood staining Johnny's shirtsleeve. He circled cautiously, waiting for another opportunity to attack on the left.

"Enough of this," Lady Throckmorton declared and, releasing Diana, edged forward. She waited for her opportunity and then wielded the ebony cane with deadly accuracy over the viscount's head. He crumpled at her feet.

Johnny looked up at her, stunned.

"Do you think we've all night?" she demanded testily.

FINLEY, with the assistance of the coachman, had bundled Brownlow into the brougham. Johnny ordered the man to drive the viscount to Dover.

He looked incredulous. "Beggin' your pardon, my lord, but that's clear the other way. We was heading north to the border. His lordship will be fit to be tied when he comes to."

"On the contrary. You may take my word for it that he will now prefer Dover," Johnny said, and pressed a number of notes into the man's hand. "I have no doubt his lordship will have a sudden desire to leave England."

"You are not simply going to allow him to leave?" Lady Throckmorton demanded, ready to do battle.

"What else would you suggest, my lady?" he asked, eyeing the cane she still carried. He wondered if it would be rude to request its return. His legs felt unaccountably weak.

"He should be punished for his effrontery!" she insisted.

"I think you may trust that he will be dealt with quite capably in France. His old friend, Lieutenant Jennot, is most anxious to settle the score with Brownlow."

"But why should he go to France?"

"He has little choice," Johnny said. "His creditors are growing impatient..." The words trailed off as the ground seemed to spin beneath him and he pitched forward at her feet.

"Johnny!" Diana cried and, disregarding all else, knelt beside him in the dirt, cradling his head in her arms. "Oh, do something!" she wailed to Finley.

The groom had already drawn his knife and with the skill of long practice, easily slit the sleeve of his master's shirt. The bandage was soaked through and he heard the young lady moan. "It looks worse than it is, miss, though he's lost a lot of blood. You untie his stock and we'll use it to fashion a new bandage. I'll just fetch the brandy."

Diana had never undressed a gentleman before, but she didn't hesitate to undo Johnny's cravat. Her hands trembled slightly as she touched his warm skin and felt his pulse beating slowly beneath her fingers.

His eyes fluttered open and he looked up to see her concerned gaze before him. "What happened?" he asked, struggling to rise.

"Lie still, my lord," she whispered, her hand pressing down on his good shoulder. "You fainted, and must not try to move just yet."

"'Faint heart ne'er won fair lady,'" he murmured, staring into her eyes. There was so much he wanted to say to her, but he felt the blackness closing in on him, and his eyes shut against his will.

"Oh, Johnny," she whispered, a tear falling on his cheek. "You have my heart, if you want it . . ."

"Here, miss," Finley said, coming up behind her with the flask of brandy. "Give him a sip of this if he comes to."

He remained unconscious while Finley changed the bandage. The groom poured a bit of the brandy into his mouth and he roused enough to climb into the carriage with Finley's support. He continued to drift in and out of consciousness, much to Diana's dismay. She urged her grandmother to have Finley stop in Kettering to fetch a doctor, but it was during one of Johnny's lucid periods and he refused.

"Time enough when we . . . reach Town. Must get you home first," he murmured before nodding off again.

When he began to snore lightly, Lady Throckmorton nodded her head in satisfaction. "He's sleeping now, child, and should recover soon enough. Let him rest until we reach London."

Diana agreed. She was content to sit beside him, and cradle his head in her lap. One hand caressed his dark, silky curls while the other gently stroked his brow. Madcap Johnny. Somehow, she should have guessed sooner that he was the Black Domino. Her heart had known, for she'd been attracted to him despite his frivolous air, but she had allowed appearances to deceive her. She had not realised the truth until that afternoon. She blushed in the dim light of the carriage, thinking of the dreadfully cutting things she'd said to him.

"Well, child?" her grandmother asked softly. "I hope you've sense enough to accept this one. He's certainly earned the right to your hand."

Diana glanced across the seat but it was difficult to make out her grandmother's features. "How did you find us?" she asked at last.

Lady Throckmorton, keeping her voice low, answered her questions as best she could, but it was not long before she, too, tired. She leaned her head back against the cushioned seat and closed her eyes. "I'll just rest for a moment," she told Diana, and then slept for the rest of the drive home.

JOHNNY AWOKE as they drove through London's cobblestone streets and was recovered enough to walk into the house unassisted. He protested he was perfectly fit, but this time Diana had her way and a footman was dispatched to rouse Lady Throckmorton's personal physician from his bed. The doctor cleansed the wound and replaced the bandage, recommended a nourishing diet and sleep, and looking half-asleep himself, quickly took his leave.

Lady Throckmorton was kind enough to leave the young couple alone in the sitting-room then, and though Violet would have remained yet awhile, she bore her daughter off with her. Diana, suddenly shy at being alone with Lord John, turned away from his penetrating eyes and played with the flower arrangement on the sideboard. So much had happened so quickly that she hardly knew what to think.

"Those roses will die in a day or two," Johnny murmured, coming up behind her.

"Yes, it is almost sinful to cut them," she said inanely, her heart racing at his nearness.

"Silk roses last a great deal longer. Now this one is not as pretty as those, and 'tis sadly crushed I know, but I had a fancy you might prefer it."

She spun round and found herself imprisoned in his arms. She looked down at the black rose he held in his hand and then up into his blue eyes. "I would rather have this one rose than ten dozen others...."

"Is it any wonder I adore you?" he whispered and leaned forward to caress her lips gently with his own. "My sweet Diana with skin as soft as any rose." He kissed her in earnest then, and she returned his embrace with all the passion he'd remembered. He lifted his head, brushing his lips lightly across her brow, before drawing her down to the sofa beside him.

She sat contentedly in the shelter of his right arm and lifted a finger to trace the outline of his jaw. "I only wish you had confided in me, my lord. I very nearly made a dreadful mistake."

"I could not, however much I wished to," he said, kissing her fingers. He smiled suddenly, a teasing light in his eyes. "Besides, dear heart, very likely you would not have believed me. You thought me such a contemptible fop."

"I will not beg your forgiveness for that, my lord—you played the part all too well!" She blushed suddenly, recalling the time she'd seen him kissing the chambermaid.

"What is it, my sweet?" he asked softly, and when she hesitated, added, "Let us have no more secrets between us."

"Oh, 'tis foolish, and I suppose just part of the role you were playing, but I was remembering that girl..."

"Poppy, do you mean?" he said with a wicked grin.

"Well, you needn't look so pleased," she said. "And I do not believe you should have foisted her off on Juliana!"

He kissed the pout from her lips and when she was near breathless and had all but forgotten what they were discussing, he smiled again. "That scene in the hall you witnessed was a demonstration of Poppy's gratitude. She had been given the sack by the landlord because she refused to accompany a guest to his room. The guest, incidentally, was your friend, Lord Brownlow."

"Brownlow! But I thought—"

"Yes, I know. Not very flattering to me, but understandable in the circumstances. I heard Poppy crying in the hall and when I got the story out of her, I offered her a place in my brother's home. She was...overcome with gratitude."

"Oh, good heavens. Your brother told me you often adopt strays, but I thought—well, you must have known what I thought."

He laughed aloud. "Not at the time, though I puzzled it out later. I admit you gave me some restless nights, dear heart."

"And all that time it was Lord Brownlow! Oh, Johnny, when I think how very near I came to marrying him—"

"Don't think it," he advised. "I never would have allowed it." He captured her fingers and tenderly kissed them, drawing a rapturous shiver from her. "Do you remember what I promised, my sweet? I swore the next time I gave you a black rose, I would claim you openly for my own."

"I remember," she whispered softly and lifted her head slightly, her lips aching for his kiss.

"Will you marry me, Diana?"

She answered him with her lips, and neither noticed the tattered rose that dropped to the floor, or the small fat pug that picked it up and waddled out the door to present it at Lady Throckmorton's feet.

"Good girl, Dulcie," her mistress said, stooping to caress the dog and retrieve the rose. She peeked once more inside the sitting room and nodded with satisfaction at the sight of her granddaughter being ruthlessly kissed. "Lord, how I envy her," she said with a sigh, and softly closed the door on Diana and Madcap Johnny.

ROMANCE IS A YEARLONG EVENT!

Celebrate the most romantic day of the year with MY VALENTINE! (February)

CRYSTAL CREEK
When you come for a visit Texas-style, you won't want to leave! (March)

Celebrate the joy, excitement and adjustment that comes with being JUST MARRIED! (April)

Go back in time and discover the West as it was meant to be . . . UNTAMED—Maverick Hearts! (July)

LINGERING SHADOWS
New York Times bestselling author Penny Jordan brings you her latest blockbuster. Don't miss it! (August)

BACK BY POPULAR DEMAND!!!
Calloway Corners, involving stories of four sisters coping with family, business and romance! (September)

FRIENDS, FAMILIES, LOVERS
Join us for these heartwarming love stories that evoke memories of family and friends. (October)

Capture the magic and romance of Christmas past with HARLEQUIN HISTORICAL CHRISTMAS STORIES! (November)

WATCH FOR FURTHER DETAILS IN ALL HARLEQUIN BOOKS!

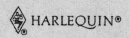

1993

The most romantic day of the year is here! Escape into the exquisite world of love with MY VALENTINE 1993. What better way to celebrate Valentine's Day than with this very romantic, sensuous collection of four original short stories, written by some of Harlequin's most popular authors.

**ANNE STUART
JUDITH ARNOLD
ANNE McALLISTER
LINDA RANDALL WISDOM**

**THIS VALENTINE'S DAY, DISCOVER ROMANCE
WITH MY VALENTINE 1993**

Available in February wherever Harlequin Books are sold.   VAL93

THREE
UNFORGETTABLE
KNIGHTS

First there was Ruarke, born leader and renowned warrior, who faced an altogether different field of battle when he took a willful wife in *Knight Dreams* (Harlequin Historicals #141, a September 1992 release). Now, brooding widower and heir Gareth must choose between family duty and the only true love he's ever known in *Knight's Lady* (Harlequin Historicals #162, a February 1993 release). And coming later in 1993, Alexander, bold adventurer and breaker of many a maiden's heart, meets the one woman he can't lay claim to in *Knight's Honor*, the dramatic conclusion of Suzanne Barclay's Sommerville Brothers trilogy.

If you're in need of a champion, let Harlequin Historicals take you back to the days when a knight in shining armor wasn't just a fantasy. Sir Ruarke, Sir Gareth and Sir Alex won't disappoint you!

IN FEBRUARY LOOK
FOR *KNIGHT'S LADY*
AVAILABLE WHEREVER
HARLEQUIN BOOKS ARE SOLD

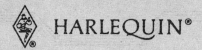 HARLEQUIN®

THE TAGGARTS OF TEXAS!

Harlequin's Ruth Jean Dale brings you
THE TAGGARTS OF TEXAS!

Those Taggart men—strong, sexy and hard to resist...

You've met Jesse James Taggart in FIREWORKS!
Harlequin Romance #3205 (July 1992)

And Trey Smith—he's THE RED-BLOODED YANKEE!
Harlequin Temptation #413 (October 1992)

Now meet Daniel Boone Taggart in SHOWDOWN!
Harlequin Romance #3242 (January 1993)

And finally the Taggarts who started it all—in LEGEND!
Harlequin Historical #168 (April 1993)

Read all the Taggart romances!
Meet all the Taggart men!

Available wherever Harlequin Books are sold.